DESERT MANNA BOOK 3

OAKS OF JUSTICE

Karen Baney

desert life
media

Oaks of Justice: Desert Manna Book 3
By Karen Baney

Publisher:
Desert Life Media, LLC
Gilbert, AZ 85295

www.karenbaney.com

Printed in the United States of America

ISBN-979-8-9858202-5-6

The Spirit of the Sovereign Lord is on me,
because the Lord has anointed me
to proclaim good news to the poor.
He has sent me to bind up the brokenhearted,
to proclaim freedom for the captives
and release from darkness for the prisoners,
to proclaim the year of the Lord's favor
and the day of vengeance of our God,
to comfort all who mourn,
and provide for those who grieve in Zion—
to bestow on them
a crown of beauty instead of ashes,
the oil of joy instead of mourning,
and a garment of praise
instead of a spirit of despair.
They will be called oaks of righteousness,
a planting of the Lord
for the display of his splendor.
—Isaiah 61:1–3 NIV

CHAPTER I

Tucson, Arizona Territory
February 25, 1873

Mel Larson walked out of the courthouse and started down the steps. The sky burned bright with the late afternoon sun. It was blistering hot.

Within seconds she was knocked to the ground. A heavy-set man with huge arms turned her over.

"I'll kill you!"

The words echoed in her mind as Calvin Westbrook straddled her with his beefy hands tight around her neck. His eyes were dark, and his brows drew together forming a deep V in his forehead.

She clawed at his hands. He only squeezed tighter. She tried to kick her legs, but his weight pinned her to the ground.

Air. She needed to get free.

She reached up and scratched at his face with all her might, tearing away three ribbons of flesh.

Breathe. No air would come. She felt lightheaded.

She struggled against the hulk of a man who murdered his wife. She could not get him to loosen his grip.

Mel's vision blurred. She was going to die.

A huge gasp. Her lungs filled with air.

Mel's eyes flew open. She was alone in the dark of her bedroom. Her soaked nightgown clung to her body as she reached for the oil lamp and matches on her nightstand. She struck a match and lit the lamp.

The soft glow penetrated the darkness. The clock on her nightstand read one o'clock. She buried her face in her pillow and cried. It had been months since her last nightmare of that awful July day four years ago.

She only worked for Virgil Pittman for a few months. It was her first murder trial. She knew early on that it would be a difficult case, even under Virgil's mentoring. Calvin Westbrook was guilty and no matter what kind of defense she and Virgil presented; no jury believed otherwise.

Mel threw back the covers and walked downstairs to the kitchen to pour a glass of fresh water. Her hands shook as she raised the full glass to her lips.

She felt silly for being so terrified of him. He was behind bars and would not get out any time soon.

After draining the glass, she set it aside. She breathed deeply of the air in her small, rented home.

She still remembered the end of Westbrook's trial clearly. When the verdict came back on the side of justice, declaring him guilty, he flew into a rage. He shook off his guard and lunged toward her. Unlike her nightmare, the scene unfolded in the courtroom. He threw her to the ground, straddled her body, and squeezed her neck until she almost passed out. It took four men to get him off her. The judge already sentenced him to life in prison, so once they got him under control, prison was where Westbrook went.

Another deep breath. Her hand finally stopped shaking.

If Mama or Papa had known about that attack, they would have yanked her back to Prescott in a heartbeat. That was why she never told them. Her job was too important.

Even if she was not legally allowed to take the tests to become a licensed attorney, she was allowed to argue cases before the court like a real lawyer as long as her mentor, Virgil Pittman, was present.

That was the only case where she had been threatened. Not one time in the four years since.

She climbed the stairs and returned to her bed, yet sleep would not come. She closed her eyes and tried to picture the lake at the ranch. Mama hung clothes on the line. Her brother Adam and his wife Julia worked with a young gray gelding in the training corral. A breeze tickled her hair as she watched the cowboys ride off to care for the herd.

Sometimes that worked. Thinking of the ranch brought her peace. She loved the years she spent there with her family.

Unfortunately, memories of home failed to push away her anxiety that night. Maybe the case she helped Junior with that afternoon was what stirred the old memories of the attack. There were similarities to the Westbrook case, a young mother murdered in her home by an abusive spouse, leaving behind a couple of small children.

Mel's stomach churned. Cases involving small children often troubled her. She wished that those children could have experienced a home like hers.

A tear slid down her cheek and she wiped it away. She glanced at the clock. Half past two.

She considered going back downstairs to reread her notes from yesterday. As soon as the thought came, she pushed it away. She needed to do her best to fall back asleep not burn through the rest of the night by filling her mind with the horrible descriptions from that case.

Mel turned on her side. She stared at her Bible on the nightstand. Without opening it, she whispered the words aloud, "The Lord is near to the brokenhearted and saves the crushed in spirit." The verse from Psalm 34 had become a favorite as well as the words a few verses later. "Affliction will slay the wicked, and those who hate the righteous will be condemned."

Lord, I don't know why I remembered that attack tonight. I know that you will slay that wicked man. Please help me sleep and find your peace again so I can give my best to our current clients tomorrow. Amen.

Mel turned down the lamp and pulled the covers to her chest as the words of those verses covered her heart.

The next morning Mel woke to sunlight shining on her face through the window. She bolted upright. Half past eight.

Oh, no! She promised Junior she would be at court by nine.

She quickly washed up and threw on her lime green dress edged with black lace on the folds of the skirt. She grabbed a handful of hair pins and tucked her hat under her arm as she ran down the stairs. She scooped up the pile of papers on her table and stuffed them into her satchel which she slung over her shoulder. As she left her home, she twisted her unruly red curls into as much of a knot as they would go, stuffing pin after pin in the mess. She placed the hat on top and secured it with several hat pins.

She looked at her watch pin. She was going to be late.

Mel hiked up her skirts and ran the last two blocks. She arrived at the courthouse at one minute 'til. Her boots clicked out a staccato rhythm as she bolted for the courtroom door.

"All rise!" the bailiff said as she dropped her satchel onto the seat between Virgil and Junior at the table for the defense. Their client was not in the courtroom.

When the judge called the court to order, she leaned over to Virgil.

"What's going on?"

He shook his head.

The judge addressed the courtroom. "Two of the jurors have been excused from the case. Since that leaves us with less than the required number, I'm declaring a mistrial."

He pounded his gavel.

"Council will meet in my chambers."

After the judge left the courtroom, Mel followed Virgil and Junior to the judge's chambers.

"Wait here," Virgil instructed.

The District Attorney joined them in the judge's chambers.

She tried to listen through the door, but she could not make out the words clear enough.

Ten minutes later, the attorneys exited.

"Bribery," Junior said. "Our client got to those jurors and paid them off."

Mel shook her head. "How did the judge find out?"

"Anonymous tip," Virgil said. "Not a solid enough connection to our client, but it was enough for the judge to act."

She sighed heavily.

"Let's regroup back at the office," Virgil said.

"I'll catch up after I grab some breakfast," she said.

Virgil raised an eyebrow as Junior continued out of the courthouse. "The nightmare?"

Mel nodded.

"Take your time," Virgil said. "Not much we can do for this case today."

Virgil hurried to catch up to his son.

The morning still held a bit of a chill, so she picked up

her pace until she reached the small café near their office. She entered and the owner greeted her. She ordered an egg sandwich to go. When her food was ready, she left and started eating as she walked.

By the time she reached the large brick building, she finished her meal. The sign on the door read: Pittman and Associates. She smiled, proud to be one of the associates. Though one day she dreamed it might say, "Pittman, Pittman, and Larson." It was a foolish thought since she was not officially a lawyer.

As Mel reached for the door handle, the hair on the back of her neck stood on end. She dropped her arm and scanned the street behind her. A wagon rolled by kicking up dust. A burly man carried a crate on one shoulder as he hurried down the sidewalk. Near the alleyway, she caught sight of someone turning into it before she could see his face.

She shook off her apprehension, vowing not to let nightmares make her paranoid.

When she entered the office, noise hit her full force. Several associates scurried to the conference room. She headed that way. One of the newest associates, Roger, handed her a cup of coffee as she entered the room. For the next hour the team theorized about what might happen with the case from that morning.

Virgil dismissed the group and she headed back to her desk.

Then she saw it. "Westbrook Escaped!" the headline read.

The porcelain mug slipped from her hand and clattered to the floor, shattering into several large pieces. Mel leaned against the edge of her desk and breathed deeply.

When she recovered, she yelled, "Who put this paper here?"

Virgil and Junior came over to her desk. Junior picked up the newspaper and started to read the article.

Mel waved her hand trying to get him to shut up. "I don't need to hear it. Who put this here?"

Her throat constricted. The man in the alleyway. Was that Westbrook?

Virgil questioned the staff, and no one saw who put the newspaper on Mel's desk.

"We have to get you out of here," Virgil said.

Her thoughts exactly.

CHAPTER 2

"Pack your bags. Junior, you go with her," Virgil barked out the orders.

Mel felt numb. Her hands tingled.

Westbrook was out. At her last encounter with him he made his intentions very clear. If he found her, he would kill her.

"I'll pick you up in an hour," Virgil said.

Junior walked with her back to her home. He kept watch while she threw all her dresses and things into her two trunks. He helped her move them near the door. By the time she finished packing, Virgil waited outside with a carriage.

"Where should I go?" Mel asked.

"Prescott," Virgil answered as Junior stowed her two trunks in the carriage.

"But you aren't leaving until Friday," she protested.

"You know me. I'm always prepared early. We'll leave on the next stage."

"What about Junior? Didn't you need more time—"

"Mel, stop. You know you are like a daughter to Eleanor and me. She would have my hide if I didn't make sure you were safe. Junior will be just fine. He's ready to take over the office. We've been planning this for months."

"But—"

"It won't hurt me to leave a few days early. I've already asked Junior to wire ahead to Eleanor to let her know I'll be there by Friday, instead of next week. She'll find a place for our 'niece,' so your name won't be on the telegram. She'll know what that means."

Mel's shoulders sagged as Virgil pulled the carriage to a stop in front of the stage station. He dropped her trunks inside the waiting area. Then he purchased tickets for himself and her.

"Virgil, this is too much. I can travel alone."

"Nonsense. You know Westbrook is a serious threat. Besides, I was going to ask you this afternoon if you wanted to help open the new office in Prescott anyway. If I remember correctly, you have family there?"

She nodded.

"Good, it's settled."

After working for Virgil Pittman for four years, she knew it was futile to argue with him. As a seasoned attorney, crafting arguments came second nature to him. She had learned so much under his tutelage and was glad that she would be able to continue learning from him, even though the circumstances driving her back to Prescott were unpleasant.

He was right. Westbrook was a serious threat. More serious than she let Virgil know. The man sent her several threatening letters from jail until she spoke to the warden about it. If Virgil would have known, he probably would have sent her away from Tucson a while ago.

As it was, she felt terrible for wrecking his plans. He planned to leave on Friday, not today. In the next four days, he had a series of meeting planned to transition the Tucson office over to his son, Virgil Pittman, Jr. Junior was twenty-eight and recently married. The plan had always been for him to take over. Virgil and Eleanor wanted to move to Prescott for years, so it was the perfect opportunity for them and it allowed Junior more independence.

However, Virgil never mentioned anything about her going to Prescott. As far as she knew, both he and Junior planned for her to stay in Tucson.

No matter. Plans shifted.

An hour later, the stagecoach carried Mel, Virgil, and their things out of Tucson away from danger. Even if Westbrook found her in Tucson, he would not know about her ties to Prescott. She should be safe there.

As dusk fell, the stage stopped in Maricopa Wells for the night. There was a small hotel, or more accurately a dirty bed in a closet-sized room where she tried to sleep.

The next day, the stage went from Maricopa Wells all the way to Wickenburg for another overnight stay. The final leg of the journey took them from Wickenburg to Prescott.

They arrived on Friday around one o'clock. When Mel alighted from the stage, someone called her name.

"Missy!"

Mel turned to the sound of her mother's voice.

"Mama?"

Within seconds both Mama and Papa hugged her close. She could not believe they were there.

"I let them know you were coming," Eleanor said when they finally released her.

"It's been so long," Mama said as she dabbed the corners of her eyes.

"Come," Papa said, "Your sisters rented a house for you in town and set it up for you."

"Would you mind if we ate some lunch first?" Mel asked as her stomach growled. She said her goodbyes to Virgil and

Eleanor, promising to check in later that day for any possible cases she needed to review.

Papa arranged for someone to deliver Mel's trunks to her new home, then he led them to a new café in town, Isabel's Café. The large windows at the front of the café were capped with red and white canvas awnings. When they entered the brick building, the hostess took them to a table in front of one of the large windows. A white linen cloth covered the table. Red and white striped napkins laid next to white porcelain plates. The server brought them tall glasses of iced water. Ice, what a treat!

Mel sipped the iced water while she reviewed the menu.

"Are they a customer?" she asked Papa.

"Yes, they buy their meat from Colter Meat Company," he said. "It's so good to have you home, Missy."

She held back a cringe. It was not that she hated the childhood nickname. She just felt like it was a name for a schoolgirl and not a successful solicitor, well almost solicitor. Someday maybe the territory would allow women, like her, to take the exams to become licensed.

"Then I'll have the roast beef sandwich with extra mayonnaise and two pickle spears." Papa smiled. He knew she picked the roast beef to support the meat company which in turn supported Colter & Larson Ranch.

Mel studied Mama and Papa while they ordered. Mama's bright red curls held more streaks of silver than she remembered. Fine lines appeared around Mama's lake-blue eyes. When she smiled, the parenthesis that separated her lips and cheeks remained after her smile faded. It was like looking into a mirror to see how she herself might look in another quarter century.

Papa's dark wavy hair thinned some and gray streaks swooped from his temples over his ears. His skin looked leathered, and sun worn, even though she doubted he spent much time with the herd anymore. His green eyes sparkled, always making one wonder what mischief he might be up to. Caroline and Adam had those same green eyes.

Papa reached over and squeezed Mel's soft hands with his large, rough one. "Are you home for good then?"

Mel smiled. "For now." She did not want to make promises she did not know she could keep.

"Eleanor said that your trip was last minute," Mama said. "Is everything alright?"

Mel hesitated. She could not bring herself to tell them about Westbrook.

"It is now that I'm here. I missed you both so much."

"I wish you would have written more," Mama whispered.

"Maggie, our little Missy is busy with very important work."

"Please, call me Mel."

Mama's reddish gray eyebrows drew together. "It makes you sound like a man. At least Melissa is your Christian name."

"Sweetheart, you will always be Missy to the family," Papa said.

Mel decided not to press the issue so soon after arriving. She loved them too much to spoil her homecoming.

"I was thinking," Mama said, "That we could have you out to the ranch soon. A big party. Your brothers and sisters and their children will want to see you."

"That would be fine." Though, the last she heard, her three sisters lived in town. Still, it would be nice to see the entire family.

Throughout the meal her parents relayed the latest family news. Caroline delivered her third child, Wade Anderson, a few weeks ago after months of bed rest. Her sister Helen moved in with her to help during that time. Mama thought Helen might move back to the ranch soon.

Mel sometimes wondered if something was wrong with her. Unlike Caroline, she had no pressing desire to marry and start breeding. If all Caroline's pregnancies had gone to term, she would have six children instead of the three: Drew, Lily, and Wade. The idea of six children before the age of twenty-five terrified Mel. She was only three years younger than Caroline and she was not sure she even wanted to marry, much less have so many children.

When they finished their lunch, Mama and Papa took her to a small two-story townhouse within walking distance from the town square. It was painted pink and had a small porch with a table and two ladder back chairs next to it. The front door was painted a deep burgundy which oddly did not clash with the pale pink house paint.

"Your sisters," Mama said, "well just Bethie and Helen since Caroline is busy with her newborn, came by and set up the house for you. It already included furniture with the rent, but they added some touches of home for you."

Papa unlocked the door and handed her the key. "Welcome home!"

She looked around the parlor and immediately fell in love with the home's quaintness. A small high-backed velvet sofa stood across from the brick fireplace. Two floral patterned chairs with flecks of the same plum color of the sofa faced each other next to two end tables that were adjacent to the sofa. The dining table only sat four which was fine with her. Most likely she would have papers spread out all over it when she brought work home. The kitchen was small, but serviceable. White frilly translucent curtains hung on all the windows.

Mama led her up to the second floor where the wash-room and two bedrooms were located. The larger bedroom included a vanity. Mel wondered if her sisters were responsible for that piece of furniture. The smaller room held a small bed which would be a nice guest room if Bethie or Helen ever decided to stay overnight with her.

"It's lovely," Mel said.

She heard Papa grunt under the weight of her trunk followed by heavy footfalls on the wooden stairs.

"There," he said as he placed the last trunk in her room. "Maggie and I will leave you. We want to get home before dark and you need to unpack and get settled."

For the hundredth time, they both told her how happy they were that she was home. She kissed them and hugged them and said her farewells before she settled into her new house.

CHAPTER 3

"Alexander!" his sister Rebecca called to him as he entered Isabel's Café. He really wished she would call him Alex, like the rest of the town did.

"I was beginning to think you would not show," she said in her sweet southern accent.

"Sorry. The judge wanted us to finish testimony before breaking for the day instead of taking a lunch recess."

"Of all days. Anyway, you are here now." She waved the server over.

Alex did not need to look over the menu. He ordered the roast beef, his favorite, with extra horseradish. When he first discovered the tangy condiment, he fell in love.

"I have some exciting news," she started. "You are going to be an uncle again!"

Alex nearly spit out his swig of sweet tea. Instead, it went down the wrong way and sent him into a coughing fit.

"Oh, my! I did not mean to startle you."

He raised a hand to stop her and slowly sipped his tea. "I'll recover."

"Anyway, I figure our child should arrive sometime in July."

Alex forced what he hoped was a genuine smile, though inwardly he was jealous. His younger sister had married, been widowed, and married again all before he found a wife. The closest he came was an eight-month courtship with Grace Talbert, now Grace Harrison. She broke it off stating that neither he nor she loved the other.

It hurt for longer than he cared to admit. He loved Grace as a dear friend. She was right to point out that there was no spark or romance in their relationship. She certainly found that with her husband and rather quickly.

Others he knew seemed to fall in love and marry, leaving Alex behind as the thirty-one-year-old bachelor longing for love and a family of his own.

He hoped Rebecca did not notice how distracted his thoughts were as she regaled him with tales of her husband and what a great father he was to her son, Josiah, from her first marriage.

If he was honest with himself, he would tell her how utterly lonely he was ever since she and Josiah moved out after her wedding fourteen months ago. He had grown attached to Josiah and looked forward to teaching him chess and other games that challenged his mind. His nephew wormed his way into his heart very quickly.

"Alexander, what is it?"

She caught him.

"I was just thinking how long it's been since you and Josiah moved out. I would love to have him over soon so we can resume our chess lessons."

Rebecca sighed and squeezed his hand. "Of course. How silly of me not to realize how much you missed him."

And that was his sister. Always kind and compassionate. Worried about everyone's heart.

He glanced over at the door as a party of three entered the restaurant. Very few people ate so late. He recognized George and Maggie Larson, long-time clients of his. Several years ago, he became the Larsons' attorney and was able to keep them on even after winning the position of District Attorney last fall. Good people.

Who he did not recognize was the stunning redhead that walked in with them. Her long red curls were pulled back on the sides and hung loosely down her back, trailing almost to her waist. Those curls shimmered in the sunlight shining through the large windows at the front of the café. Her figure was perfectly proportioned and curvy.

Alex reached for his sweet tea when his mouth suddenly felt dry.

"Who is that with George and Maggie?" Rebecca asked. She must have caught him staring.

"I don't know." But he wished he did. He had never seen the woman before. He would have remembered her.

"Perhaps we should introduce ourselves."

Alex glanced over at them. Clearly George and Maggie were close to her, by the way they touched her hand. "I think they are in the middle of a long conversation. Better not to interrupt."

Then his heart nearly stopped. She laughed and looked directly at him. From across the room, she must have sensed his stare. He quickly looked away. Then he glanced back to see if she still watched him. She did not.

"She reminds me of Maggie," Rebecca said. "Very similar coloring and facial features. Maybe she is Missy, their second daughter, a few years younger than my friend Caroline. Though Caroline did not mention her sister was coming for a visit."

Alex pushed away his half-eaten sandwich, suddenly feeling the urge to run back to the solace of his office. He could easily make up an excuse to leave without offending Rebecca. Yet, a part of him was reluctant to leave.

"Why don't you have supper with us after church on Sunday? Bring your chessboard. I am sure Josiah would love to see you again," Rebecca said.

"I'd like that."

Rebecca excused herself to return home to finish some chores. He still felt guilty for not bringing her to Arizona sooner. They had grown up surrounded by wealth. He went off to law school and then moved to the West while his mother, Rebecca, and her son became paupers. No one told him until years later. By the time he brought her and Josiah west, she was used to life without servants. He tried to find her a wealthy husband, but she chose love and hard work instead.

He sighed as the server wrapped up his half-eaten sandwich. Then he paid for the meal and headed back to the District Attorney's office. Though he would have preferred the quiet of his private practice, he still had business to attend to.

Since Prescott was relatively small, it was common practice for the District Attorney and his associates to maintain some clients through their own private practices. He kept many of his clients, knowing if there were ever any conflicts of interest, he would have to sever the relationship. In the four years he lived in Prescott, no District Attorney faced that dilemma.

When he opened the front door of the two-story brick building, noise assaulted his ears. His assistant district attorney, Harrold Blankley, leaned over the shoulder of one of the legal assistants. They were in deep discussion but paused when he entered the room.

"We have a break on the Jose Gutierrez murder," Harrold said. "I filed the paperwork against Oscar Molina this morning while you were in court. We have eyewitnesses that place him at the restaurant where Gutierrez was last seen alive."

"Good."

"Pretrial starts Monday."

The timeline seemed fast to him. It would not give opposing council much time to prepare.

"Who is the attorney for the defense?" Alex asked, figuring he should go meet with him to make sure he was ready for the case.

"Mel Larson from Pittman and Associates."

Alex frowned. He knew Virgil Pittman moved to town and opened an office with a few associates, but he had yet to meet Mr. Mel Larson.

"I'll head over to meet with him now. Anything I should know before I go?"

"Here's a copy of the filing for the defense."

Alex took the paperwork and put it in his briefcase. Then he walked the short distance to Pittman and Associates.

When he entered the wood clapboard building, his eyes adjusted to the lower light. There was no one at the front desk or in the waiting area so he walked down the hall. As he neared the library, he heard papers rustling, so he entered the room. Bookshelves lined the walls full of legal books. A long oak table took up the center of the room with eight chairs surrounding it.

His breath caught. The redhead from lunch sat at the table with several legal books open. She held a pencil and took notes as she read. She was so focused on what she read that she did not notice him, so he studied her more closely.

Her long red hair looked darker in the lower light of the library. Faint freckles dusted her cheeks and nose. Her face was long, more of an oval shape and her narrow nose rounded at the tip. He thought it might be nice to touch it.

"Love the law?" he teased.

She jumped and looked up at him.

"I'm sorry, I did not mean to startle you."

Her eyes swept over his hair, face, beard, and chest before locking with his eyes. He felt heat climb up his neck and settle into his face. Thank goodness his beard hid his neck. It was probably bright red. Then she smiled broadly. It was a nice smile that lit up her entire face.

"Yes, since you asked. I do love the law."

"And why is that?"

"The law is black and white. It provides guideposts for how we treat each other. It is the mark of a civilized society. Without it we would be doomed to be barbarians."

He laughed. "I suppose that is one way to look at it."

"Do you not agree?" She laid down her pencil and stood.

"Nothing you said was inaccurate. However, the law is so much more. I don't think it is quite as black and white as you would believe. If it was, why would we need juries?"

She crossed her arms over her chest accentuating her feminine figure. He swallowed hard. Then she tapped a finger to her chin.

"It seems you make an excellent point."

Virgil entered the room. "Good afternoon, Alex or should I say, Mr. District Attorney? I'm sorry my secretary did not greet you."

Alex shrugged it off. He found it odd that Miss Larson was pouring over legal books in the library rather than manning the front desk. It still took some getting used to seeing female secretaries. More law firms in town hired them. He still preferred Bradley Whitaker, his secretary. He was a very organized man with an extreme attention to detail and a keen mind.

"What brings you by?" Virgil asked.

"We filed a motion for trial against your client, Oscar Molina, for the murder of Jose Gutierrez." Alex handed over a copy of the paperwork. "My assistant tells me you have a Mel Larson who will be representing him?"

Miss Larson coughed and took a sip of water. Virgil glanced over at her, and she shook her head.

"Yes, Mel and my firm represents Mr. Molina."

"Will you be ready for pretrial on Monday?"

Virgil glanced at Miss Larson again.

She spoke up, "Yes, Mel Larson will be ready for pretrial on Monday."

"Alright, I'll see you in court on Monday," he said shaking Virgil's hand. "Good day, Miss Larson."

Alex caught another strange look pass between the attorney and his secretary. Something was off but he could not put his finger on it.

CHAPTER 4

Mel let out a long breath.

"What was that all about?" Virgil asked.

"He thinks I'm your secretary. I never gave him my first name."

Virgil cocked his head to one side. "Oh, I see where this is going."

"You and I both know our client is innocent and the crux of this case is mistaken identity from what you told me earlier," she said. "What better way to illustrate this point to the court than to show that our esteemed District Attorney is as susceptible as the next person to mistake someone's identity?"

Plus, it would put him in his place. Of course, he would assume she held the lowest position possible at the law firm. She had no qualms about exploiting his narrow mindset to prove a point.

"Are you sure you want to do that, Mel? He is the District Attorney."

"Yes."

"Alright. For this to be fully effective, you're going to have to sit in the gallery for jury selection and let me lead it."

"That is an excellent idea."

"I know we just got into town today, are you sure you

don't want to head home to rest. We can pick this up tomorrow."

"We need all the time we can get to prepare," she said, even though she knew tonight would be a late night. She did not expect to have a case so soon.

"Virgil, how did my name get assigned to this case? I was not even supposed to be in Prescott."

"You weren't?" He winked at her. "Let me go get some coffee and paper."

He turned and headed down the hall to his office, leaving Mel to wonder if he always intended to bring her there. He had been in Prescott in early January to get Eleanor settled and hire some staff. He must have submitted her name at that time. There was no other explanation for it.

"How long have you known about this case?" she asked when he returned.

"Mr. Molina came by when I was here in January, so I knew it was a possibility that we would go to trial shortly after moving here. This is certainly sooner than I expected."

Virgil brought her up to date on the details of the case from his meeting with Mr. Molina. Then they both reviewed the motion for trial. She read a copy of the investigator's report. Her eyes snagged on one very important detail.

"Listen to this, the eyewitness said that it was someone named 'M.O. or O.M.' who was at the restaurant and was last seen with the victim."

Virgil frowned.

"I told you. My gut was right. This is a case of mistaken identity. None of the witnesses mention Oscar Molina by name. Just the initials M.O. or O.M. I think our District Attorney has the wrong man."

"We need an investigator to dig deeper on this tomorrow. Do you know anyone who would be a good investigator?"

"Yes. There's a cowboy out at my father's ranch. Name is Hawk. If you send word out to the ranch that Missy," she rolled her eyes, "Larson needs his help, he'll be here first thing in the morning."

Virgil found the only associate who was still in the office and sent him off to Colter & Larson Ranch to find Hawk.

The next morning, Mel arrived at the office early. Virgil arranged for Mr. Molina and his wife to arrive by ten o'clock. Prior to then, Mel wrote out a series of questions on several sheets of paper, leaving space for her to write their answers.

After hours of questioning her client and his wife, Mel found that Mr. and Mrs. Molina had dined at the restaurant that evening. Then they went straight home together. Mrs. Molina confirmed that at no time was her husband out of her sight that evening. She mentioned it was their anniversary.

By three o'clock, Hawk joined her and Virgil in the office with his report.

"Some witnesses remember a man matching Oscar Molina's description. They say he dined with his wife and left the restaurant by eight o'clock that night. Neither Oscar nor his wife had anything stronger than tea."

Hawk continued, "There was a Manuel Ortiz at the restaurant that night. He drank several shots of tequila and a few other drinks. He was known to have been confronted by Jose Gutierrez about his wife on several occasions. It seems that Ortiz had been seen with 'his hands all over' Mrs. Gutierrez several times. Gutierrez initiated a fight that night. Both left the restaurant after the fight, still fuming over it, according to witnesses."

"Excellent work!" Virgil said. He took a copy of Hawk's report and paid him. "In the future, if we need similar help, would you be available?"

Hawk agreed, then took his leave.

"Hopefully your father isn't upset over us stealing away one of his men for the day."

"It won't be a problem."

Mel yawned and her stomach growled. It was seven o'clock. She had not eaten all day.

"You should head home to Eleanor," she told him.

"And you should go get some food and rest."

She gathered her papers and placed them in her satchel. As they left the office building, Virgil gave her one warning.

"Don't work on Sunday or stay up too late on this tonight. It's pretty cut and dried. We know who to call to the stand to get this case thrown out."

Mel nodded. She thought about heading home, but realized she still had not purchased any food. So, she went to Isabel's instead.

The server led her to a dimly lit back corner of the room. She ordered a meal then pulled out several papers from her satchel to read. Only her mind would not focus. She kept thinking about when she first met Alex Glassman yesterday afternoon. He was perhaps the most handsome man she ever met. He was nearly a foot taller than her. She thought his long beard and flyout waxed mustache gave him an intelligent appearance. His eyes were a peculiar color. She still could not decide if they were light brown or gold. When he smiled, his beard rose with his grin and little lines formed around the corners of his eyes.

Too bad he underestimated her. She felt his condescension the moment she answered his question: *Love the law?*

Why was it so hard for men like Alex to understand that women like her were intelligent and capable of doing the same work as men? He was the opposite of Virgil in that regard.

Which led her to her quandary. Should she use his assumptions about her against him in her opening statements? It would be relevant to the case, but there were other ways of proving her point that her client was on trial due to mistaken identity. She could present the point in a way that did not make a potential enemy out of the District Attorney. At the same time, she felt like he almost deserved it.

Sadly, Virgil was no help in that matter. He would support her no matter what. Sometimes she wondered if he let her take an audacious approach just to throw off opposing council. Other times, she found he allowed her to do similar things so she would learn a valuable lesson.

She crossed her arms over her chest and tapped one finger on her chin. If only she knew which way Virgil thought, she might be able to avoid a painful lesson.

She put her papers back into her satchel and studied the diners in the room. There were only a handful of people. A young couple flirted and kept finding excuses to touch each other's hand or arm. An older couple talked in hushed tones. A group of three men listened on the edge of their seats to their friend's animated tale.

"Is this seat taken?"

A very tall man stood over her. She recognized the walking stick with an ivory handle immediately, but she allowed her gaze to travel up to his face.

"Mr. Glassman." What was he doing there?

"May I join you?"

Her heart picked up pace. "If you are here to ply me with questions about Virgil's strategy for the case, then—"

"I'm here because I noticed you sat alone. I thought you might like some company."

Just then the server came out with her meal. She held another meal in her hand which she set down opposite Mel. She frowned as Alex took a seat.

"Shall I say grace?" he asked.

She bit her lip. It would be much harder to go with her strategy in court if she got to know the man. But he was very friendly and easy on the eyes.

Mel motioned her hand across the table letting him know he could sit.

She watched him as he said grace then felt a little guilty for not taking the prayer to heart.

"I haven't seen you around town before."

"I just moved back."

"You're George and Maggie's daughter? Missy, right?"

Mel took a bite of her food and chewed slowly. His gaze locked with hers. He would be a valiant opponent. She swallowed.

"Yes."

He took a bite of his food and narrowed his eyes for a few seconds. Then he smiled. "Welcome home."

Clearly, they were going to have dinner together, so she might as well be polite. "Have you been the District Attorney for long?"

"No. I won the election last fall and started my term in January."

"Ah, so you're still wet behind the ears." She held back a smile. That was good news for her. She tended to do well in court against newer DAs.

He laughed. "Hardly. I've been an attorney for almost a decade now."

"Yes, but being an attorney is far different from being a

DA."

He narrowed his eyes. "How long have you been Virgil's secretary?"

Never, she thought. "I've worked with Virgil for four years."

"Down in Tucson, then?"

"My, how observant you are." She took another bite of her meal to keep herself from getting snarky.

When he took another bite of his meal, she saw her opportunity to change the subject. "How long have you been in Prescott? I don't recall the name Glassman."

"Since late 1869."

"I see. I left in early 1869 for Tucson. Do you have family here?"

He smiled. "My sister and her son moved here a few years ago. She is remarried. The house feels pretty empty now."

Mel's heart snagged. He was lonely. That's why he sat down. He saw her by herself and probably assumed she was lonely too. She made an effort to be nicer.

The conversation grew easier and before she realized it, an hour passed, and she enjoyed the time with him. He was a nice man. Interesting. He told her stories about his nephew and his antics. It was going to be very hard to stick with her strategy in court.

"Shall I walk you home?" he asked.

Mel stiffened. "I would not want to put you out."

"It's no trouble."

She consented and they walked in companionable silence until she arrived at her doorstep. "Good night, Mr. Glass-man."

He smiled at her. "Good night, Miss Larson."

She opened the door and stepped inside. She closed the

door. While she lit a lamp, she looked out the window and noticed he waited until her lamp was lit before he continued on his way home.

Mel leaned her forehead against the door. It would be so much easier if he was a brute or oaf or very unpleasant.

CHAPTER 5

Alex arrived to church a little earlier than normal before Rebecca arrived. He spotted Missy taking a seat with her parents and sisters. She noticed him and smiled. He waved back and smiled as his heart felt lighter.

He took a seat in his usual pew. While he waited for Rebecca and her family to arrive, he studied Missy Larson. She smiled and engaged with her unmarried sisters. When her oldest sister arrived, she greeted her with a hug, and she took great interest in each of the Anderson children.

She would be a good mother, he thought as he watched her crouch to their level and ask them questions.

Rebecca cleared her throat. "So, you've met her then? Or are you still in the relentlessly staring at a stranger phase?"

Alex's face warmed. "I joined her for dinner last night."

It was a half-truth. He manipulated his way into sitting at her table when he noticed she sat alone. He could tell when he first showed up, she was more annoyed than anything else. As the evening went on, he thought she warmed up to him. He certainly enjoyed her company.

Rebecca did not say anything else. Alex greeted her husband and son just before the service began.

Throughout the service, his eyes traveled over to where Missy sat. She listened intently to the pastor's sermon. She appeared to sing with gusto for several songs.

When the service ended, Caroline Anderson dragged Missy toward their pew.

"Rebecca, come meet my sister, Missy." Caroline introduced her to Rebecca's family including Alex.

He chose to take Missy's hand in his and gave her a light kiss on it. "Pleasure to see you again."

Missy's cheeks turned bright red. Her voice was impassive. "Alex."

The light green dress she wore complimented her fair skin and pleasing figure. He admired her taste in clothes.

After a few awkward seconds, Caroline moved Missy along to meet some other friends.

"We'll see you at home," Perry said to Rebecca. "We need to go feed my horse."

She kissed her husband on his cheek then turned her full attention to Alex.

"You are still having dinner with us, right?" she asked.

"We can dine at my house," Alex countered. "There's more room."

"Nonsense, I already have a roast in the oven. It will not take but a few minutes to make some collard greens." She glanced down then looked up at him with a sweet smile on her face.

"That look may work on your husband, but it does not work on your brother."

"Whatever do you mean?" She asked as she hooked her hand through the crook of his arm and tugged him in the direction of her home. "Besides, I learned a few tricks from Cookie before... Well, before we all started our new lives," she said brightly. "Including your favorite."

"I do not believe you. There is no way you know how to make Cookie's blackberry pie."

"Well, you will just have to wait until after dinner to

34

find out."

As they entered her simple home, Alex frowned. It was a far cry from their ornate childhood home of Maple Grove Manor. It was incredibly plain compared to his grand home a few streets over.

Her home was half the size of his. The parlor held only four chairs and two side tables that surrounded the large stone fireplace. A plain light oak table with spindled legs sat between the parlor and the kitchen. He had never seen the bedrooms but judging by the size of the rest of the house, they must be small.

"Have a seat," she said pointing to one of the six chairs around the table.

"I could not help noticing you noticing Missy Larson."

Alex's face warmed. "And what of it?"

"Alexander, she is nearly a decade younger than you."

"So was Grace. What is your point?"

"Her older brother, Adam who runs Larson Stables is younger than you." She turned away from the simmering collard greens and wrote something down on a piece of paper by the table. "That reminds me, I need to make an appointment with him this week. Perry told me about how he trains the ranch horses to handle the cattle. The way he describes it, the horses almost appear to dance with the cattle. Anyway, would you not like to see such a thing at the Independence Day celebration?"

"Fascinating," he muttered hoping she would leave off the earlier conversation. Independence Day was four months away. But that was Rebecca. Always planning.

She rubbed her lower back. "We could use the corral at the freight company so Perry and other cowboys can demonstrate this 'dance'. His horse is stabled up at Thomas's livery and he has been practicing. It is so good to see him in a saddle again."

"I thought your husband was a teamster."

"Oh, he is and probably will remain so. But he does miss horses. I suppose sometimes he even misses ranching."

She stirred the collard greens and checked on the roast in the oven.

"About Missy Larson—"

"Do not start," he warned her. He loved his sister dearly and even enjoyed their verbal sparring from time to time. Unfortunately, she knew how to provoke him, and he sensed that was where the conversation was headed.

"You need to understand she is very well connected in this community. Her father, George Larson is Will Colter's partner and the 'Larson' of Colter & Larson ranch. Her brother, Adam owns Larson Stables. Her sister, Caroline, is my truest friend. They have a great deal of power and influence in this community. Don't trifle with her."

Best not to tell her the Larsons were clients of his. "I do not trifle with women, Rebecca."

She sighed. "I suppose not. She's just so young."

And beautiful, he thought. Those dark red curls and flashing blue eyes both frightened and exhilarated him at the same time.

"Uncle Alex!" Josiah greeted him and jumped on him to deliver a hug.

Rebecca frowned and cleared her throat.

"—ander," Josiah finished his name.

"You do not have to be so formal," he said hugging his nephew back.

"Alexander." Rebecca's voice held an edge, so like Mama's warning tone.

"Please, Rebecca. I'm trying to be less formal these days and more approachable to the townspeople of Prescott. As their District Attorney, I want them to feel like they can trust me and that I am on their side. Besides, you are the only person who calls me by my full name."

"You do not need to shorten your name to do so. They elected you did they not?"

Alex frowned.

When Perry entered the room, the conversation turned to other topics and by the time the meal was over, Alex was glad he came, no matter how quaint his sister's home was or how stern her warnings were about Missy.

As he walked home, he wondered if Missy would be in court during the murder trial. His secretary only came to court when something urgent arose. He supposed she would stay back at the office. Too bad. He would like to have occasion to talk to her, even if it was before court and during breaks.

He shook his head. He only just met her. It was so unlike him to be taken so quickly. He needed to be careful. Maybe Rebecca was right after all. Maybe he should not pursue Missy Larson.

CHAPTER 6

Monday morning Alex arrived at court with Harrold. They took their place at the table closest to the jury box. A pool of jurors waited outside the courtroom for the bailiff to escort them in.

Virgil sat at the other table in the courtroom, dressed in a plain brown suit with a vest. The man was skinny and short, though not quite as short as Missy. He did not appear the least bit nervous that Mr. Larson had not yet arrived.

Alex glanced around the gallery. Missy sat on the bench immediately behind Virgil. He smiled at her. She nodded. She wore a bright blue dress edged with cream lace with a high neckline.

The judge entered the courtroom and took his position on the bench. He motioned to the bailiff to bring in the potential jurors. The judge asked a few questions of each juror before allowing Alex to question the jurors.

Most of the potential jurors were white, but the few Mexicans amid the number he saw as assets. The victim was Mexican, after all. Virgil also asked questions of the jurors and did not object to any of the jurors that Alex selected. Mr. Mel Larson never did show up.

It was too easy. Something did not make sense, but he could not put a finger on it.

They finished the selection by noon, so the judge excused them for the day. Alex looked for Missy as he left. She was already gone.

The next day in court Alex felt confident about his strategy.

As the judge entered the courtroom, Alex looked around for Mel Larson. No such man appeared. Missy sat next to Virgil at the defense's table wearing a lime green dress that nearly stole his breath away.

The judge started the trial and Alex stood and began his opening statements.

"The prosecution will prove beyond a reasonable doubt that Mr. Oscar Molina murdered Jose Gutierrez on the night of December thirtieth outside of the Mexican restaurant on eighth street. During the night, Mr. Molina was seen conversing heatedly with Mr. Gutierrez. Eyewitness testimony will show…"

Alex made the mistake of looking at Missy. She narrowed her eyes. Her arms were crossed over her chest emphasizing her pleasant curves while she tapped a finger on her chin. He wondered if she had any idea what that pose did to a man.

Harrold shuffled some papers noisily, rousing Alex from his thoughts.

"Eyewitness testimony will show that Mr. Molina was the last person to see Mr. Gutierrez alive."

Harrold nodded, indicating that he thought Alex had said enough to sway the jury. So, Alex took his seat.

When Missy Larson stood and walked over to the jury, his stomach plummeted to the floor. Missy. Melissa. Mel.

He frowned as she delivered her opening remarks.

———

Mel purposely crossed her arms over her chest when Alex looked at her. Was it juvenile? Yes. Would Mama be disappointed? Yes. Was it clever? Yes.

When he sat down, she stood and walked over to address the jury. She faced Alex and noticed the color drain from his face. She knew the exact moment when he realized who she really was. Heaven forgive her for what she was about to do.

"Gentlemen of the jury. My name is Mel Larson."

Alex's eyebrows furrowed deeply as he glared at her.

"I am a member of the defense team for Mr. Molina. While I am not a licensed member of the court, I am permitted to argue this case before you today under the supervision of Virgil Pittman, who is a licensed member of the court.

"Now, I am sure many of you thought to yourself, just as our esteemed District Attorney did, that I was perhaps Mr. Pittman's secretary or even a member of Mr. Molina's family and not part of his defense team.

"That, gentlemen, is what this case boils down to in its simplest form."

She locked gazes with Alex. "Mistaken identity."

He glared at her. She noticed his fisted hand in his lap. She hit her mark and it wounded him, perhaps more than she intended.

"The prosecution will present a very compelling case against the murderer of Jose Gutierrez. Many of the facts they will present are accurate and damning. Unfortunately, the prosecution has the wrong suspect."

"Objection!" Alex shouted and stood to his feet. His chair tumbled to the ground with a loud thud.

She turned her back to him. She goaded him to the point of breaking procedure. He would hate her for it later.

"Mr. Glassman!" the judge yelled. "Sit down. You cannot object to opening statements."

"Request to approach your honor," he said.

"This is highly irregular, Mr. Glassman. Sit down and allow Ms. Larson to finish her opening statements. Then we will confer in chambers during a short recess."

Alex growled but took a seat.

"Ms. Larson, you may proceed."

"Thank you, your honor. As I was saying, the prosecution has the wrong suspect. The defense will prove that Mr. Molina was at home sleeping next to his wife during the time of the murder. We will prove that, while Mr. Molina and his wife dined at the restaurant in question on the night in question, they were not a part of the scuffle between Mr. Gutierrez and the murderer. We will also prove that Mr. Molina did not have any personal connection to the victim.

"This is a case of mistaken identity. Someone who looks a little like Mr. Molina and shares similar initials is the likely suspect, not our client."

Mel took her seat at the defense table. As promised, the judge ordered a short recess and instructed all council to chambers.

Virgil explained what happened to Mr. Molina.

Mel stood and started towards the judge's chambers at the same time as Alex, nearly colliding with him.

"No, after you, *Mel*." The acid dripped from his voice. She may have gone too far. She made it personal.

CHAPTER 7

Alex followed Missy—Mel—whatever her blasted name was. Virgil and Harrold were close on his heels.

When they entered the judge's chambers, Alex started to speak but Judge Henderson instructed them all to sit down.

"I will not have my court mocked. Mr. Glassman, what got into you? You're the District Attorney for goodness's sake!"

"Your honor, this... this... This..."

"Woman?" Mel offered.

He turned to her and gave her the most disgusted look he could muster. "This woman is not a licensed attorney. What is more she made a mockery of my position and the court. She volleyed a personal attack that was unfounded."

"Was it unfounded?" Judge Henderson asked. "Or is this really about your ego, Mr. Glassman? You were called to the carpet for your prejudice towards what roles a woman might hold."

"Your honor, she is not licensed."

"That is correct, Mr. Glassman. She is not legally permitted to be licensed at this point in time. It is only a matter of time before she and other women like her receive that opportunity. However, she is permitted by precedence to argue the case as long as Mr. Pittman oversees her work both in the courtroom and outside of the courtroom."

Alex's pulse raced. His face heated. His stomach churned. He knew he did not have a leg to stand on, and it added to his frustration and anger.

"Doesn't the territorial law state that a person representing someone in court must be 'a *man* with some level of legal knowledge.'"

"Do not attempt to school me on the law, Mr. Glassman." Judge Henderson spat out his name.

"As I have already stated, there is precedence for Ms. Larson arguing this case. It is a precedence this court will uphold."

Alex started to stand.

"Sit down!" the judge yelled.

Harrold grabbed Alex's arm and whispered, "You need to calm down."

"We will adjourn for today to allow the District Attorney to regain his composure. Ms. Larson, in the future, you will refrain from dragging the District Attorney or his position into the case, be it in opening statements, during the trial, or closing remarks."

"Yes, your honor," she replied.

"You may all get out of my court now."

Alex stood and threw the door open so hard it bounced off the wall and started to close on Harrold. He stormed into the courtroom and grabbed his things then left and waited for Mel Larson outside.

When she stepped into the daylight, he stormed toward her, glad that his height would feel intimidating to her.

"What the hell was that, Missy? Mel. Whatever!"

She stepped closer to him and looked up and met his gaze. Her wide eyes blinked as a coy smile spread across those full lips. "That is what you call a coup d'état, Mr. Glassman. Or you can call it a well-crafted argument if you'd like."

Darn it all, if he did not love and hate her at the same time in that moment.

He growled and stormed back to his office, barking at Harrold the whole way. "Put one of the associates on the legality of a woman arguing a case in court within the Arizona Territory."

"You heard the judge," Harrold said. "There is precedence. I believe Mel Larson is a huge part of that precedence. From what I uncovered this morning, she has been arguing cases for Virgil Pittman down in Tucson for four years now. She has a very strong success rate too."

"That would have been helpful information three hours ago!"

"Don't you think you are overreacting a bit?"

"No."

Alex opened the door to his building forcefully. Harrold caught it before it did any damage. He stormed down the hall to his office and slammed the door behind Harrold.

"Look, Alex, I know it bruised your ego to have a woman call you out—"

"In open court!"

"But she may have a point. What if we have the wrong man? Isn't that a valid question to ask?"

Alex glared at Harrold. "If we have the wrong man, then someone is getting fired from this office and it won't be me. Go do your job and make sure we have the right man or file the paperwork to end this case!"

Harrold sputtered.

Alex yelled, "Get. Out."

Harrold closed the door behind him as he scurried off to his desk.

Alex pounded his fist down on his desk. Of all the low

tactics she could have used, she chose to drag him through the mud. And to think he was attracted to her and even thought for a moment he might want to get to know her. Some darn fool he was.

He took a few deep breaths to calm his rage. Then a few more. His angry outburst toward Mel and then his staff was too reminiscent of his father. He wanted to be a better man than Solomon Glassman.

If he was an outsider looking into this case, he might consider her unconventional strategy rather smart. She hit her mark with perfect aim. Before one lick of evidence was presented, she convinced the jury that her client was innocent, that the DA's office made a mistake, and that he was a curmudgeon with archaic ideals.

It was brilliant.

Alex stroked his beard. A knock sounded on the door.

"Sir," Bradley ventured. "Would you care for some coffee?"

Alex motioned his secretary in. "Got anything stronger?"

"Sir?"

"Never mind. Coffee is fine."

Bradley set the mug on his desk. "Can I get you anything else?"

"No, thank you."

Alex sipped his coffee thinking through how he would undo the damage to his case. He completely underestimated Mel Larson. That was his mistake and his alone. Hopefully his staff did not have the wrong person. If they did, it would be a blow to the office and to him.

With any luck, the facts presented would clear up any confusion over Mr. Molina's guilt or innocence and justice would prevail.

CHAPTER 8

Mel smiled as Alex walked away. She executed her plan flawlessly.

"I would not smile if I were you," Virgil warned. "You may have made a dangerous and powerful enemy."

"I thought you were in favor of my approach."

"To a point, but you took it over the top, Mel. It may be a bridge you cannot cross again."

Her shoulders sagged as her smile faded. If Virgil was disappointed, he probably had good cause.

"Remember when you speak, you do so on behalf of my firm. I do not want our reputation to be one that has people questioning our honesty. That stunt may have men thinking that we would stoop to theatrical tactics to sway the jury, instead of swaying the jury with clear facts. We just have to prove reasonable doubt, not burn down the system."

Mel swallowed the lump in her throat.

"Go home. I'll meet you back in court tomorrow. When the prosecution rests, I may take over the defense. I haven't decided."

Mel blinked rapidly. She disappointed him. She could take Alex screaming in her face or a murderer choking her in court more than she could bear disappointing Virgil.

"I'm sorry," she whispered, willing her eyes to stay dry.

Virgil's voice softened. "Go home, Mel. We will turn

this around."

She nodded and walked down the street in the general direction of her home. A little part of her wanted to go cry on Caroline's shoulder. She wasn't one for a pity party.

Mel opened the door of the townhouse and tossed her satchel on the chair by the door. Then she flopped onto the upholstered high back sofa, replaying the morning in her mind.

What a disaster. She let her ego get the better of her. She could have presented her point strongly without personally attacking Alex. That evil part of her enjoyed seeing him squirm for underrating her. She wounded him. That was unprofessional and mean-spirited, two traits that would disappoint her parents as well.

She hoped that Virgil would let her continue with the case, despite her mistakes. She really wanted to help Mr. Molina, especially since he was innocent.

Despite the early hour, she went up to her bedroom and laid down on her bed. She barely slept since she arrived in Prescott, so she took a nap.

When she woke, it was four o'clock in the afternoon. She adjusted her hair and headed toward Caroline's house.

As she knocked on the door she heard a loud crash, so she opened it.

"Chase me, Lily!" her nephew Drew teased his little sister.

"I get you, Doo," three-year-old Lily yelled as she bumped into an end table, nearly knocking over a lantern.

Caroline held a crying baby Wade in one arm but managed to scoop up the oil lantern from the end table before it fell.

"Dexterous like a cat," Mel said.

"Missy!" Caroline exclaimed as she placed the lantern

back on the table. "Drew, Lily, come say hi to your Aunt Missy."

The two children skittered to a stop in front of her.

"Please call me Mel," she said. Caroline frowned.

Lily looked up at Mel with her green eyes and blond hair. "Hi, Aunt Mel!"

Then she squeezed her leg with her little arms.

"Hi, Lily. You are as pretty as your mama."

"Hi, Aunt Mel." Drew came over and hugged her around her waist. At six and a half years old, he could easily reach her waist, unlike little Lily.

"You look more like your papa every day."

He puffed out his chest as his blue eyes twinkled. She tousled his sandy brown hair before he darted off.

Caroline excused herself for a moment to change Wade, then she returned to the kitchen.

"Would you mind holding him while I fix supper?"

Mel took baby Wade in her arms. A strange sensation washed over her as she noticed his softness. His eyes were green, like Caroline's. It was hard to tell if his hair would be blond like hers or sandy brown like Thomas's. She breathed deeply and found that she liked clean baby smell. She held up a finger and he squirmed.

"He's so tiny."

Caroline laughed. "He's a newborn still. Give him a few months and he'll look chubby and even cuter. So, what brings you by?"

Mel sighed. "I made a huge mistake in court today."

Then her story tumbled out with all the gory details of her failure.

"The worst part is that I can't decide if I'm more ashamed of disappointing Virgil or injuring Alex—er, Mr. Glassman."

Caroline looked up from peeling the potatoes. She studied Mel. Then she grinned.

"You like Alex."

Caroline chopped the potatoes as if she had said something far less profound, like the sky is blue.

Mel shifted Wade to her other hip.

"You can put him in the bassinet." She nodded toward it.

Mel gently laid him down and kissed him on the top of his head. He was the most adorable creature she had ever seen.

After asking how she could help with supper, she asked Caroline, "What makes you say I like Alex?"

"That."

"What?"

"You go all soft and gooey when you say his name."

"I've only just met him."

Caroline snorted. "I know you did not live here yet when I met Thomas or when Adam fell in love with Julia. Surely, you've seen friends fall in love? Or think about Papa and Mama. We spent our whole lives watching what a couple in love looks like in good times, bad times, fun times, and sad times."

Mel found some canned beets in the pantry and brought them to the table as Caroline fried the potatoes over the stove. Mel dumped the beets into a pan and set it on the stove to warm.

"Would you like me to make some dessert since you'll be staying for supper?" Caroline asked.

"I don't want to put you out."

"It's no trouble. It will cook while we eat. Besides, Thomas and Drew would prefer if we had dessert every night."

50

Mel laughed.

"I think you should apologize to him."

It took Mel a minute to follow Caroline's train of thought. "I don't know where Alex lives."

"Oh! I do. I'll give you directions after supper. It looks like a miniature plantation house. You can't miss it."

Mel sighed. Caroline was right. She should apologize. Tonight. Before sitting across from him in court again. She owed him that much after being so impertinent.

When Thomas arrived home, he greeted her.

"She goes by Mel now," Caroline said as she scrunched her forehead. "Guess she wants to sound more like a man."

It was true, so Mel let it slide.

They ate supper together followed by a lovely apple pie for dessert. Then Caroline gave her that look.

"It's getting late and you have somewhere to be," Caroline said before giving her directions to Alex's house.

Mel memorized the directions, though it sounded like he only lived a few blocks away. She said her goodbyes to her nephews and niece then headed toward Alex's home.

When she was a few houses away, she spotted it and it was just as Caroline described. It had a long porch that ran the length of the house. White pillars stood strong and made it feel like a plantation house. The brick material gave it a stately appearance. Each window was flanked with shutters.

Mel walked up the porch steps and proceeded to knock on the door. When Alex greeted her, his frown spoke volumes.

CHAPTER 9

At seven o'clock, Alex decided to sit in the parlor and read. Only he could not concentrate. Though his anger calmed, he still felt hurt by the disaster in court that morning. A part of him dreaded what Mel Larson might do in the coming days. He should not worry, as he would dominate the case the next day, presenting evidence against Mr. Molina. The worst she could do was ask a few questions of his witnesses. The evidence would speak for itself.

A knock sounded on his door. He set aside the book he failed to read. Then he stood and opened the door.

"Mel." Her name flew from his lips with a sarcastic flair.

She wrung her hands together. "May I come in."

Alex stood there and visualized slamming the door in her face. Only he would not be so rude. Nor did he care to invite her into his home.

"Caroline tell you where I live?"

She nodded. "How did you know?"

"She is your sister. And she is my sister's best friend. Not too hard to figure that out."

She wrapped her arms around her waist. She was nervous. A little part of him was glad.

His shoulders dropped as he caved. "Please have a seat," he said pointing to the chairs and porch swing as he stepped onto the porch.

She took a seat on the porch swing. He angled a chair to face her. Then he waited.

It was dark outside and chillier than he thought. She shivered. Good. Maybe she'd make it fast.

The light from the fireplace inside the parlor illuminated one side of her face, casting a golden glow onto her red hair. She did not wear a hat or a coat, he noted.

"If it's about the case, you know we cannot talk about that."

"It's not. Well, not exactly."

He frowned.

"I owe you an apology."

Alex schooled his expression trying to appear impassive even though he inwardly felt surprised. If a man had treated him the way she had, that man would not be on his doorstep apologizing.

"I realize that what I did was hurtful when I used you as an example. I could have made my point clearly and effectively without bringing you into it. I know I wounded you and I am sorry."

Alex stiffened. She had wounded him. Deeply. More than she could know. The few times he had seen her prior to court, he was drawn to her. Her beauty captivated him even when he was not around her. So, when she pulled that stunt in court, the knife hit a part of his heart he tried to protect. He was used to being unloved, so to have opened his heart a tiny crack to Mel only to have her do that... It hurt.

"I am sorry to have disturbed your evening."

She stood abruptly. Her foot caught on the front hem of her dress, and she stumbled forward.

He jumped to his feet and caught her arms before she fell. The air between them sizzled and sparked like the fire burning in his fireplace. He loosened his grip slightly, so as not to harm her.

As he studied her eyes in the dim light, he thought of several scenarios that could happen next. He could so easily slide his hands down to her waist and press her body to his, capturing her lips with his mouth. It would only take a slight movement from him to start.

Or he could back away and send her home.

Or he could kiss her and explore her back with his hands.

She did not move or breathe.

He did not want to move for fear he would give into the temptation of her. His breathing shallowed. He needed to do something. His gaze dropped to her lips, her full beckoning lips.

"Thank you," she whispered.

His eyes snapped back to hers. He released his hold and stepped back. "I accept your apology."

Still neither one of them moved. The tension in the air eased but did not fade.

Then she suddenly smiled. "I do hope we can be friends after this trial is over."

Before he could respond, she dashed down the stairs of the porch and headed back to her home.

He stood there for several minutes. At first, he debated if he should walk her home. Then he stood there in stunned silence afraid of his own desire for her. He should be angry. He should hate her. He should not have let her off so easily.

Yet, one look into her eyes and it was obvious she felt something too.

Grace had been right last year to break off their courtship. There was no spark. She called him out on it. She had been right.

He went back inside his house and sat near the fire. He supposed the lack of attraction in his relationship with Grace was what kept him from ever proposing. Deep down he wanted something more, just like Grace had.

Alex's stomach tightened as he imagined what kind of mess his heart would be in had he married Grace and then met Mel. Thankfully, he had been spared that predicament.

Despite the morning's wounds, he resolved to fully forgive Mel. He respected her bravery for coming to his home to apologize. No man would have done that. Even most women would not have done that. It showed that she was a woman of principle and that she valued mending fences when she was in the wrong. It took a certain humility to apologize like that.

Alex stroked a hand over his long beard. Then he stood and poured himself a glass of whiskey. It was going to be hard to get through the trial sitting so close to her. Watching her as she worked. He would watch with new appreciation starting the next day. He downed the last of his drink and headed to bed.

———

Mel's heart raced when Alex grabbed her arms to steady her. The fire that moved through her body at his touch unnerved her. She had never been kissed before, but she was sure he wanted to, especially when he stared at her lips. She could only imagine what a kiss would have been like given her strong reaction to his touch. She wanted that kiss.

In the end, her common sense prevailed. She could see the struggle in his eyes and knew it would be up to her to break the tension before he did something foolish to jeopardize his career. It had been a calculated risk to go to his house since they were on opposing sides of a case. She needed to clear her conscious and make things right before the next day. But, if anyone had seen her there, it could have caused trouble for him.

She let out a long breath and resisted the urge to look over her shoulder to see if he still stood outside. She did not want him to see how deeply he affected her.

She rubbed her hands on her arms against the chill. She should have brought a shawl or coat with her.

As she walked home, Mel wondered if Virgil would let her proceed with the case or not. He was right to be disappointed with her. He invested a lot of time, energy, and money into mentoring her. She would be his primary litigator until he hired more staff. As such, she represented his firm with every word and argument she uttered in court. She owed him an apology in the morning.

She opened the door to her townhouse and stepped into the cold dark room. After lighting a lamp, she built a fire in the fireplace while her teeth chattered. Once it was started, she sat with a shawl wrapped around her arms and stared into it.

Mel wondered what Alex was thinking at that moment. Was he affected by that touch as much as she had been? A small part of her hoped he thought of her and that he meant what he said about accepting her apology. She would hate to miss out on something potentially great because of her mistake.

After a while, she headed upstairs and slipped under the chilly covers of her bed, warmed by the memory of the evening.

CHAPTER 10

Two days later, Alex continued his arguments against Mr. Molina.

"The prosecution calls Edgar Ramirez to the stand," Alex said.

Once Mr. Ramirez was sworn in, Alex proceeded. "Mr. Ramirez, where do you work?"

"I own the Mexican restaurant on eighth street."

"Do you also tend bar at your restaurant?"

"Si. I know all my regular customers."

"On the night in question, December thirtieth, do you recall seeing the defendant at your restaurant?" Alex stepped to the side so Mr. Ramirez could get a clear look at Mr. Molina.

"Si. He came in around seven o'clock with his wife. They sat at a table away from the bar."

"Did you notice anything else about Mr. Molina that evening?"

"Around eight o'clock he was sitting at the bar and Jose Gutierrez came up to him and yanked him off a bar stool. The two men started swinging at each other. I kicked them both out of the bar and stood in the street until they went their separate ways."

"Thank you, Mr. Ramirez. No further questions."

Judge Henderson looked at Mel as Alex took his seat.

"Your witness, Ms. Larson."

"Thank you, your honor."

Mel stood and smoothed out the folds of her skirt. She wore a simple chocolate brown high collared dress with no embellishments, save for an ivory cameo pin where her collar came together. She fashioned her hair very conservatively, twisted into a chignon at the base of her neck. Alex held back a smile when he noticed little wisps of curls along the edges of the twist. Her hair could not be tamed any more than she could.

"Mr. Ramirez," she started, "you mentioned that Mr. Molina sat on a bar stool around eight o'clock. Where was his wife?"

Alex wrote a question mark on a piece of paper and slid it over to Harrold. Harrold shrugged. Mel's question was good, and his team should have thought of that.

Mr. Ramirez stammered. "I... I..."

"Is it true that you do not know where Mr. Molina's wife was because the man at the bar was not really Mr. Molina?"

"I... I... don't know."

Alex frowned. It was such an important detail and his team missed it. He missed it.

"One last question. Mr. Ramirez, did you witness the actual murder of the victim, Jose Gutierrez?"

"No."

"No further questions, your honor. The defense reserves the right to recall the witness during our arguments."

The judge granted her request. She lifted her chin and took her seat at the defense table as the judge excused Mr. Ramirez.

Alex's palms sweat with each witness he brought. Mel asked the same two questions of each person who witnessed the fight at the bar, and she reserved the right to recall each one. What did she know that he and his team had missed?

With each subsequent witness, Alex had to admit she certainly caused him to have reasonable doubt. If he doubted Mr. Molina's guilt, the jury would too. Perhaps they really did have the wrong man.

When the judge called recess for the day, he instructed Harrold to meet him back at his office. Then he stopped by Isabel's and ordered dinner for the whole office. He wanted answers to Mel's questions. Isabel agreed to have a young man deliver the food as soon as it was ready.

Alex walked the few blocks back to his office. He was disappointed, but he also wanted to make sure they had the right man.

"Listen up!" he said as he entered the main office area. "Where was Mrs. Molina during the fight?"

Blank stares greeted him.

He already knew that none of the witnesses saw the murder, so he did not press them on that point.

"As you know, the fight between Molina and Gutierrez was the foundation of this case. Our witnesses' testimony puts Mrs. Molina with her husband 'at a table away from the bar' as Mr. Ramirez testified to during court. So where was Mrs. Molina when the fight broke out?"

A few associates shuffled through some papers. They came up empty.

"Who interviewed Mrs. Molina?"

Again, blank stares.

"People!" Alex stroked his beard for a few seconds as he tried to calm down. "Do we have the right man?"

At that moment the food arrived and was set out on the long table in the center of the room.

"Eat up! Then I want you to pore over everything we

have on this case to find out where Mrs. Molina was and confirm if we have the right man or not. Harrold, my office."

Alex strode into his office and when Harrold entered, he motioned him to the seat across from his desk as he closed his door.

"We are not sending an innocent man to prison. That will not happen on my watch. If we are completely wrong on this, I have no problem asking for a mistrial or withdrawing the case."

Harrold nodded.

"But we should not be in this position. This was a critical detail. The sheriff should have interviewed the defendant's wife."

He already knew the defense's strategy. Mel would present character witnesses the next day to show how upstanding Mr. Molina was. His wife would confirm his alibi. No one saw him murder Mr. Gutierrez. Nothing connected Mr. Molina to Mr. Gutierrez beyond a reasonable doubt.

"This is a huge mess, Harrold."

"Alex, no one in this office has prosecuted a murder trial before. Most of these men haven't attended law school, like you have. I, myself have, but certainly not one as prestigious as Harvard."

"Your point?"

"We were trying to figure it out as we went. Come on, Alex. We usually prosecute theft and petty crimes. This is only the second murder trial prosecuted by the District Attorney's office. None of us worked here for the first one.

"Did we miss a critical detail? Yes. It's unfortunate," Harrold finished.

"It's more than unfortunate. Do you understand that a man's reputation and livelihood are at stake here? How would you feel if it was you on trial up there?"

"I'm not Mexican."

Alex's blood boiled. Of all the ridiculous things to say. "Get out."

Harrold stood and left the room, closing the door behind him.

He did have one good point—it was Alex's fault. He assumed his staff would challenge the facts and dig deeper than they had. He failed as a leader to recognize how ill-equipped they were for their jobs.

Alex kept them until eight o'clock, when they presented him with no new information. Then he let them go, knowing Mel would shred him in court the next day, as she should.

CHAPTER II

Friday dawned with streaks of pink and orange in the sky. Mel rose and donned her emerald green dress. She wore her hair pulled back on the sides and trailing down her back. It never seemed to cooperate when she put it in a chignon.

She checked her appearance in the full-length mirror next to her vanity. It was her favorite dress and complimented her complexion well. She always felt confident wearing it.

Mel went downstairs and grabbed her satchel before heading over to Isabel's. She ate at least one meal a day there, so she finally asked Isabel yesterday if she would be willing to make her an egg sandwich to eat on the way to court or the office most mornings. The kind woman eagerly agreed.

As she entered the café, she spotted Isabel behind the counter in the back. She smiled and Isabel held up one finger. Mel nodded.

"Here you go," Isabel said as she handed over the egg sandwich. "I put some cheese on it. If you want me to adjust anything, just let me know."

"Thank you," Mel said as she handed her a few coins.

When she stepped out onto the street, a warm voice greeted her.

"Morning, Mel."

She waited for Alex to catch up.

"Morning." She smiled up at him.

He smiled down at her. Little lines formed in the corners of his eyes. Then he frowned as she took a bite of her egg sandwich.

"What's that?"

"An egg sandwich." She took another bite.

"Never heard of such a thing."

She tore off a piece and handed it to him. He frowned at it and refused to take it. She raised it to his lips. "Just try it."

Finally, he opened his mouth and she stuffed it in. He chewed the bite slowly then a smile spread across his face.

She caught the scent of his cologne. He smelled good. Manly. It made her face warm.

"It's good. Is it something new at Isabel's?"

"I asked her to make it. The café by the courthouse in Tucson made them. Many of the attorneys bought them on the way to court. Junior was the one who introduced me to them."

"Junior?"

"Virgil's son, Virgil Pittman, Jr. He took over the Tucson office when Virgil moved here last week." She could hardly believe that was only last week. "Anyway, I described it to Isabel, and she agreed to make it for me in the morning. I much prefer this over buying eggs, cooking, and cleaning up all before court. It saves me so much time, especially if I've had a late night preparing."

"Were you up late last night?" he asked as he held the courthouse door open for her.

"No. This case is easy." She winked at him. "See you in court."

"I'd wish you luck, but I have a feeling you don't need it."

She smiled before she hurried down the hall to meet Virgil.

"Chummy with the District Attorney this morning?" Virgil asked.

She told him she apologized to him on Monday night and smoothed things over. Virgil decided to let her argue the case after that.

"He ran into me on the way here."

"You ready?"

"Of course," she said as she entered the courtroom.

"I figured. If you brought out the emerald dress, I know you're ready for the kill."

Mel snorted. "Am I that consistent?"

Virgil laughed. "Yes."

A few minutes later, Alex and Harrold Blankley arrived. Within minutes the judge started the proceedings for the day.

"Mr. Glassman, do you have any further witnesses?"

"No, your honor. The prosecution rests."

"Ms. Larson, you may proceed."

"Thank you, your honor. The defense would like to call Mrs. Molina to the stand."

Once Oscar's wife was sworn in, Mel smiled and hoped Mrs. Molina remembered her instructions from the night before.

"Mrs. Molina, can you tell us about your dinner at the Mexican restaurant on the evening of December thirtieth?"

Mrs. Molina took a deep breath and smiled. Good job, Mel thought.

"It was our fifth anniversary. Oscar surprised me that morning with a bouquet of flowers and a note that he would take me out this year. We never go out to supper, so it was a real treat. I put on my best dress and fixed my hair the way he liked it. When he came home from the mine, he even bathed before we went out."

Red tinged Mrs. Molina's cheeks.

"What time did you arrive at the restaurant?"

"Around seven o'clock. Oscar asked for a table away from the noisy bar. It was so romantic. We ordered enchiladas with a dark mole sauce. It's my favorite."

"It sounds like you had a lovely time. What time did you and Oscar leave?"

"It was around a quarter past eight, after we saw a fight break out. Oscar did not want me around that."

"Can you tell me about this fight?"

"Si. Oscar and I just finished our dessert when we saw a heavy-set man, he was Mexican, storm into the bar and yank another skinnier man off a bar stool. He spoke in Spanish, accusing the skinny man of... How do you say it?"

"Sleeping with his wife?"

"Objection. Leading the witness," Alex said.

"Overruled," Judge Henderson replied. "You may continue Mrs. Molina."

"Yes, he said the skinny man slept with his wife." Mrs. Molina's face turned red.

"What happened next?" Mel gave her an encouraging smile.

"Mr. Ramirez threw both of them out of the restaurant when they started fighting. Oscar took me home."

"And I know this is an embarrassing question, Mrs. Molina, but were you with Oscar all night, especially around half past one in the morning?"

"Si." Her face bloomed red. "We were together all night."

"Is there any chance that Mr. Molina could have left after you fell asleep?"

"No. It was our anniversary. We did not sleep much that night."

Poor Mrs. Molina. Mel wished she could squeeze her hand but knew it was against procedure.

"Thank you, Mrs. Molina. No further questions."

"Your witness, Mr. Glassman," Judge Henderson said.

"No questions, your honor."

Mel frowned at Alex. No questions at all. She expected him to come up with something.

The judge excused Mrs. Molina.

"Ms. Larson, your next witness."

She mouthed "trust me" to Virgil as she decided not to parade the slew of character witnesses in front of the court. Her gut told her she did not need to. She was going in for the kill.

"The defense would like to recall Mr. Ramirez to the stand."

As Mr. Ramirez took the stand, Virgil nodded to three skinny Mexican men who looked similar to Oscar Molina. They took a seat on the bench behind the defense.

"Mr. Ramirez, as you just heard testimony from Mrs. Molina stating that she and her husband were still at their table when the fight broke out between Jose Gutierrez and another man, can you tell the court with absolute certainty the other man was indeed Oscar Molina?"

She stepped out of the way so Mr. Ramirez could get a good look at Oscar and the three men behind him.

"I... I really thought it was him, but now I am not so sure."

"Do you see the man who fought with Mr. Gutierrez in the court today, even in the gallery?"

"No. He looked like Mr. Molina, but I don't think it was him after all. I'm sorry."

"No further questions."

Alex frowned at her. She could tell by the slump of his shoulders that he knew he lost. She was not quite done yet.

When Alex declined to redirect, she called Sheriff Smith to the stand.

"The defense would like to enter exhibit C into evidence at this time." She took a copy to the judge and then to Alex before presenting her copy to the witness. She waited for the judge's approval before continuing.

"Sheriff Smith, can you tell the court what this document is?"

"Yes. It is my report of the investigation of the murder of Jose Gutierrez."

"Can you read this underlined section here?" she said as she pointed to the report.

"The witnesses describe the man at the bar as a short Mexican man in his twenties. Skinny. Long mustache, but no beard. He was often seen at the restaurant alone and drinking heavily." The sheriff cleared his throat as he saw his mistake revealed.

"And can you read the second part that is underlined here?"

She heard Alex cough behind her, presumably as he read the most damning evidence of Mr. Molina's innocence.

"The bartender, Mr. Ramirez stated that the man's initials were something like M.O. or O.M."

"M.O. or O.M." Mel repeated for affect. "Is it possible, Sheriff Smith, that the suspect's initials were 'M.O.' and did not match Oscar Molina's initials of O.M.?"

The gallery filled with loud whispers. She glanced over her shoulder at Alex. His face was red.

"Answer the question, Sheriff," she said.

The judge banged his gavel. "Order! I will have order in

my courtroom."

"Is it possible that the suspect's name goes with the initials 'M.O.'?" she repeated the most relevant part of the question.

"Yes." The sheriff swiped a hand over his face.

"No further questions."

Mel turned on her heel and marched back to the defense table. She watched as Alex stood and admitted he had no further questions.

Her mouth twitched as she held back a smile. She won.

She stood. "The defense rests."

"Let's take a short recess before we proceed with closing arguments."

"Your honor," Alex said. "May we confer in chambers?"

He nodded.

Mel and Virgil asked Mr. Molina to stay in the courtroom as they joined Alex, Harrold, and Judge Henderson in chambers.

Alex started, "Your honor, the prosecution would like to drop the charges and case against Mr. Molina. As Ms. Larson has deftly pointed out, Mr. Molina's identity was mistaken for the actual suspect, though we have yet to determine who he is. As such, the District Attorney's office would like to clear Mr. Molina's name and apologize to the court."

"Ms. Larson?"

"We accept."

"Then I will address the court now."

They returned to the courtroom and the judge threw out the case due to insufficient evidence that Mr. Molina was the perpetrator and that he believed Mr. Molina was wrongly charged with the crime.

Mel held back a smile as Alex openly apologized to the

court and to Mr. Molina for his office's mistake.

"It's over," she said to Mr. Molina. "You are free to go."

Mr. Molina left with his wife.

"Should we tell him that he could sue the District Attorney's office for defamation?" she asked Virgil.

"No. I don't think he wants to ever set foot in a courtroom again. Besides, Alex did the right thing."

"If you are fine with it, I'll gather our investigation and notes and turn them over to Alex this afternoon," she offered.

Virgil nodded.

Mel walked out of the courtroom with her head held high. She helped Mr. Molina get justice. And she won. It always felt a little good to win.

CHAPTER 12

Mel gathered the large stack of notes into a crate and carried them over to the District Attorney's office. When she arrived, Harrold Blankley greeted her.

"Is Mr. Glassman here?"

"No. He's over at his private office just down the street. You can't miss it. Can I take this for you?"

"Yes. It's our notes from our investigation. I'm sure Mr. Glassman will find the information helpful in hunting down the real killer."

Harrold took the crate into Alex's office as she turned to leave.

Mel stepped out into the mild March day. The sun warmed her face as she lifted it out of the shade of her hat. She had not realized how much she missed Prescott. The climate was a little cooler than Tucson and far less dusty. The air always smelled fresh and often held a hint of pine or juniper. She sighed. It was good to be home.

Home. The next day she would ride out to the ranch for the big party Mama planned. She did not welcome all the fuss over her, but she was eager to see everyone at the ranch. It was over four years ago since she saw them all. She imagined many things were different. Her nieces and nephews would be taller and older. She wondered if Adam had any sons yet. Surely, they would have written with that news.

She turned down Goodwin Street and quickly found Alex's firm. "Glassman, Attorney at Law," she read the sign aloud.

Mel entered the brick building and waited for her eyes to adjust to the dim light. Dark wood wainscoting covered the lower portion of all the walls. Sconces shown a soft glow on the burgundy painted walls. It was regal and elegant, like the exterior of his home. He had no qualms about showing off his wealth.

She studied the large landscape painting between the two sconces for several minutes. She loved how the artist captured the beauty of Granite Lake with its brilliant blue water and stark grayish white stone against the backdrop of a cloudy sky. The scene was familiar to her, as her family picnicked by the lake on several occasions. She scanned the lower corner for the artist's name. "A. Glass..." She could not make out the full last name, but it had to be Glassman.

A noise sounded from her right, but she continued to stare at the painting.

"Do you like it?" Alex whispered as he joined her.

"It's mesmerizing. You captured the essence of the lake. The detail of the rock formations is so accurate. Where did you learn to paint like that?"

"What makes you think it's mine?" He asked as he leaned against the wall and watched her. He crossed his arms over his chest, making it look even broader.

Mel raised an eyebrow. "Do I really have to answer that?"

"I'd like you to."

She looked at him then. His golden-brown eyes sought her approval. She was taken aback. Clearly the painting was important to him.

"One, it is meticulously detailed, like what I might expect from someone who dresses equally meticulously."

"I'm meticulous?"

"Are you fishing for compliments right now?"

"Maybe. I suffered a pretty big blow to my ego this morn-ing and am still trying to recover."

She ignored his comment when she noticed the hint of a smile near his eyes.

"Two, the signature, although it fades after the second 'S,' clearly it says 'A. Glassman.' I'm guessing you don't have any relatives in the area whose name begins with 'A'?"

He shook his head. "What else?"

"Third, it is from the local area. Very wise choice for your office, by the way. I am sure your clients feel more at home because of it. Anyway, it means someone local paint-ed it."

"And?"

"And it's hanging on your wall for pity's sake." She turned to face him and propped her hands on her hips tiring of his sparring.

"You win again. Congratulations on the case, by the way."

He motioned her to follow him into his office.

She hesitated for a moment when she realized there was no one else in the building. He left the door open and rounded the corner of the largest walnut desk she had ever seen. She supposed a tall man might need a bigger desk. Or perhaps he enjoyed being a bit showy.

Mel took a seat across from his desk.

"Did you come by to gloat?" he asked softly as he took a seat behind his desk.

"No. I just came from your office. Your other office. We dropped off our notes from our investigation. I believe the man you are looking for is named Manuel Ortiz. He had been spotted with Gutierrez's wife on more than one occasion."

"Thank you."

She watched him as he studied her. After several seconds he looked away.

"Thank you for keeping an innocent man out of prison. I'm very disappointed that I did not catch our mistake. I see now that I have a lot of mentoring to do with my staff and need to be more involved in the operations, especially on such an important case."

"Thank you for admitting the mistake and getting the case thrown out. Most of the DAs and ADAs I worked with in Tucson would never have done that. They would rather the jury decide so they could maintain their pride, especially if I was on the other side."

He looked at her again. "You are a remarkable woman."

She smiled as his compliment settled into a special place in her heart.

"You never said if you liked it."

Mel quirked an eyebrow.

"The painting."

"I love it. It brought back memories of picnics with my parents and sisters before I moved away. Do you have others?"

He nodded.

"May I see them?"

"Perhaps another time."

She smiled. He seemed suddenly shy about his artwork. "Where did you learn to paint?"

"I painted as a child and young man." His wistful expression turned cloudy. "Until my father found out. He destroyed a good many of them in a fit of rage, tossing them into a bonfire in the backyard."

"Oh!" Her heart ached for him. What kind of father would do such a thing?

"He told me that no son of his would be an artist. He felt it was a demeaning pursuit."

He stopped abruptly and stood. He crossed the room to a buffet and poured himself a drink. When he lifted a second glass to her, she shook her head. He took a sip before he returned to his desk with his glass.

Mel's heart was sad. It was clearly a painful memory with a longer story. She wished she could carry some of that pain.

"Are you busy tomorrow or Sunday?" she asked impulsively.

He took another sip of his drink and eyed her over the rim of the glass. "No. Why?"

"My family is having a welcome home party for me out at the ranch. I would like it if you came too. Might be nice to get some fresh air and sunshine." She smiled broadly despite the nervousness that caused her hand to shake. She hoped he said yes.

"What time should I pick you up?"

His face was impassive. Could he not show some excitement?

"Seven?"

He nodded. Then he stood and rounded the corner of his desk and escorted her to the front door.

"See you tomorrow," she said as she left and headed home, more than a little excited to spend the weekend with Alex.

———

Alex let out a long breath as Mel left. He had a lot to sort through in his mind.

He glanced at his painting as he walked by. She was the first person to ever study it long enough to realize he painted it. The way she looked at the painting had nearly undone him. He watched the different emotions cross her face. Joy probably from seeing a familiar place. Nostalgia when she made a personal connection. Awe at the technique as she stepped closer. Surprise when she saw his signature.

How many friends, family members, and clients walked past that painting over the years. Most ignored it. A few glanced at it. One or two stopped to look at it. No one studied it.

Yet she had for several minutes. And she seemed hesitant to leave it. She did not just study it. She experienced it.

He let out a shaky breath as he sat down at his desk and sipped his whiskey.

It unnerved him.

He painted the scene when he first moved to Prescott from San Francisco four years ago. Something about Prescott and the surrounding area reignited his artistic passion that his father tried to destroy.

The Granite Lake painting, which he called 'New Life,' embodied all the hope in his soul. Sure, it was a detailed and accurate depiction of the scene. It was also his soul on canvas.

For Mel to have experienced the painting almost as he did—it was as if she saw his soul on that canvas, even if she had not realized it.

He turned over the paper on his desk that he started before she arrived. It was a drawing of her from court that day. The life in her eyes when she looked over her shoulder at him stuck in his mind's eye and he wanted to capture it on paper.

After taking another sip of his whiskey, he picked up his

pencil and refined the sketch. It was the moment he knew she won. She had never looked more beautiful than then. He rubbed the pencil shading to smooth over the shadow on the paper, so it looked more like the shadow cast on skin. He filled in more detail of the curls of her hair, that silky, spunky, curly hair.

When he was satisfied with the drawing, he stared at it for several minutes. Any animosity he felt at the beginning of the trial or by being bested by a woman had faded. He saw the most amazing woman he had ever met.

She was courageous in taking on the bias of men, like himself, towards women. She was extremely intelligent as evidenced by her flawless research. She even knew who the real suspect was. He shook his head. She was kind and humble in the right moments, like apologizing to him the other day or even a few minutes ago by sharing her research. She never teased him about having the wrong man. She only stated facts in a compassionate way.

Alex stroked his long beard. Then he downed the last of his whiskey and headed home. It had been a long day and it sounded like he would have a busy weekend ahead.

He tapped his walking stick on the board sidewalk as he walked down the street. She asked him to meet her family. He already knew her parents. Did she realize how significant her request would appear to them? To him?

After reserving a carriage for the morning, he finally made his way home. As he sat down at the large empty table in his quiet house, he thought about his personal dreams. His professional dream was realized in his position as District Attorney, though he clearly had more to learn.

On a personal level, he was tired of living alone. He wanted a wife. He wanted children. He wanted to see a slew of smiling faces at supper staring at him. For the first time, their faces started to take shape. A little girl with curly red hair and lake-blue eyes. A little boy with dusty brown hair and brown eyes. A wife with fiery red hair and a fierce ambition who loved him enough to put up with all his flaws.

He sighed as he pushed his half-eaten meal away. Maybe the weekend at the ranch would be a turning point for him and Mel. Maybe she would see him as a potential husband rather than an opponent in court. He prayed so.

CHAPTER 13

The next morning, Alex donned his light gray slacks, a crisp white shirt, and a silver scarf-style tie which he tucked into the top of his vest. He wore the silver cuff links from Mama. Then he donned the matching light gray suit jacket. He slicked his hair parted to one side and brushed his long beard before waxing the tips of his mustache, so they were perpendicular to his beard. He looked over his hats and decided the gray bowler would be more practical for a day outdoors. He glanced at his walking stick and decided to leave it behind. Though he did enjoy using it, he figured it was a little over the top for a day at the ranch.

He left and picked up the carriage from Thomas Anderson's livery. Then he drove to Mel's house to pick her up. He knocked on her door.

When she opened the door, she smiled. Then her eyes rounded.

"I did mention we are going to the ranch, right?"

Her outfit looked so out of place compared to what she wore in the courtroom. She wore a flowing white shirt cinched at the waist with a brown leather belt. He tightened his jaw so it would not drop open as he studied the tan western split skirt. He had seen other ranch women wear something similar, but that did not seem like his Mel. A cowgirl hat rested on top of her loose wild red curls. He wanted to run his fingers through them.

She grabbed his arm and pulled him inside her parlor. "Have you been to a ranch before?"

"Of course. I have clients down in Peeples Valley and Congress." He did not understand what she was upset about. He wore what he normally would to a client on a ranch.

She paced back and forth in front of him, her loose curls bouncing with each click of her... Were those cowboy boots? Who was the wild western woman in front of him?

"This won't do. Don't you have any denim pants or work trousers? Or something more casual?"

"No."

He swallowed hard as she stepped closer and narrowed her eyes.

Then she began undressing him! She grabbed his jacket and tossed it on a nearby chair.

"Wait!" Did she have any idea how expensive that was?

Then she untucked his neck scarf from his vest. She smelled like juniper and cinnamon. His heart picked up pace as she untied his neck scarf. He grabbed her wrist.

"What are you doing?" His voice was husky and betrayed him.

"I am," she jerked her wrist free and waved her hand in his face, "trying to make you look less like a stuffy attorney and more like someone on a ranch, although I'm not sure how. At least I'll make you look less stuffy."

When she reached for his neck scarf, he ripped it off and tossed it on top of his jacket. She set his bowler hat aside. Then she ran her hands down his arms sending fire coursing through his veins. He held his breath.

"Relax. I'm almost done."

He took a deep breath, and the juniper fragrance filled

his lungs again, only making it more difficult to stand so close to her and not pull her into his arms and kiss the sass out of her.

"These are very nice," she said as she removed his cuff link. She held it up to the light. "We'll take good care of those."

She set it on the end table on top of a lace doily.

"They were a gift from my mother when I graduated from law school."

His heart felt like a stampeding herd within his chest or at least how he imagined one might feel.

She rolled up the cuff of his shirt, once. Then twice. Then three times. Then her soft fingers left a trail of fire behind as she pushed it up just over his elbow. When she removed the other cuff link and did the same with his other sleeve, he caught her hand before she pulled it away.

Her gaze met his. In that moment she saw the effect she had on him, and she stepped back.

Her voiced cracked as she spoke. "That will have to do."

Mel grabbed a valise which he took from her.

"Ready?" she asked.

He held the door open for her. When she passed by, her wild hair bounced with each step. It was so full and puffy around her head. No wonder she usually wore it pinned on the sides.

He set the valise on the porch and took her key and locked the door. Then he gave her the key back, picked up her valise, and led her to the carriage.

"Oh. A carriage."

The sardonic tone of her voice let him know he somehow let her down.

"I figured you did not want to walk all the way there."

"No, no." She squared her shoulders and did not wait for

his help up into the carriage.

When he sat down, he became all too aware of how small the seat was as his thigh brushed up against hers. He set the carriage in motion headed out of town toward Colter & Larson Ranch.

"Should I have rented some donkeys? Or perhaps a wagon?" he teased.

"Now I would like to see the meticulous Alexander Glassman on the back of a donkey. If I ever did, I would be sure to memorize the scene as it would bring me laughter for years to come."

Sass. He laughed.

"I guess I was expecting two horses. I am a ranch girl after all. Been riding since before I was tall enough to reach the stirrups."

"Is that so? I wasn't quite sure if you were tall enough to reach them now."

"Very funny. What I may lack in stature I make up for with intelligence."

"And sass." He hadn't meant to say it out loud, but there it was.

She laughed loudly and from the belly for a good minute. "My mama and papa would agree with that."

"They are clients of mine, you know."

"Really?"

"Yes. One of my earliest clients when I moved here. George had been using the same attorney as Will, but he thought it seemed wise for them to have their own just in case anything ever came between them. Adam is a client as well."

She glanced up at him and her wild hair brushed against his exposed forearm. He was not sure he would make it through the weekend a sane man if his body kept reacting so strongly to everything about her.

"The Colters and Larsons have been friends for decades," she said. "Back in Texas, Edward was good friends with Papa almost from the beginning. Papa moved there after he met his Irish princess—that would be Mama, of course. Edward and Catherine were a little older than Papa and Mama. Catherine already had Reuben and Will when they met.

"Anyway, I won't bore you with our entire family history. Suffice to say we have been friends for a very long time. Especially, Caroline and Julia. They were born a few months apart. Even more ironic is that their first-born children were born on the same night within hours of each other."

The carriage crested a hill and gave a stunning panoramic view of the ranch.

"Oh, stop here, please."

He studied her. The excitement in her eyes was contagious. He found himself smiling along with her as he pulled the carriage to a stop. She got out of the carriage and spun around in circles.

"Isn't this the most beautiful place on earth?" she asked.

"Yes," he said not taking his eyes off of her. He secured the horse then exited the carriage and went to stand next to her.

"Look way out as far as you can see. That's the herd."

He saw them but moved closer and leaned down. "Where?"

She extended her arm and pointed again. He rested his chin on her shoulder. He heard the air leave her lungs.

"There," she whispered.

The sound of a wagon came up behind them and Alex stepped away.

"Hello there!" Thomas Anderson greeted them. "I wish

you had said you were coming out here. I could have saved you some money and we could have all ridden in the wagon."

"Thomas, I don't think they would have wanted to ride with an old married couple and three children," Caroline Anderson said.

Alex greeted them both. Mel continued to stare out over the ranch.

"What's wrong with her?" Thomas asked.

"We'll see you down there. Come on, Thomas, let's leave them to enjoy the view," Caroline said as she winked at Alex. She knew what was what.

As they pulled away, Alex returned to Mel's side. He debated if it would be too forward to put his arm around her. He decided he would try.

When he did, she put her arm around his waist and snuggled close. Though he was nearly a foot taller than her, he thought that she fit perfectly there at his side.

CHAPTER 14

Mel sighed as Alex put his arm around her. She quite enjoyed the feeling of his side pressed against hers. In fact, there were a number of things she enjoyed about the morning so far.

She held back a laugh as remembered how he showed up in a suit looking all spiffy for a weekend at the ranch. She thoroughly enjoyed making him squirm as she adjusted his wardrobe... Until she saw that look in his eyes. Was that what passion looked like? She was not sure, but she was both a little frightened and a lot excited about it.

Taking a deep breath, she forced herself away from the warmth of his side. His hand slid down her arm and captured her hand in his.

"Everyone can see us up here. They will be wondering why we are taking so long."

"Let them wonder." His voice was husky again which sent pleasant tingles up and down her arms.

"We should go."

"If we must," he said as he led her back to the carriage.

A carriage. She smiled as she sat in the seat. "Can you ride?"

"Of course."

The way he scrunched up his face said a lot.

"You can but you don't really like it?"

He sighed. "I can and have. When I make the rounds to my clients down in the valley, I always ride. It's just not my favorite thing to do. I end up walking funny for a few days after."

Mel outright laughed at that. "Perhaps you need some tutoring or more practice."

"Are you offering?" He smiled down at her as he started the carriage forward.

"Maybe."

"It's bigger than I expected," he said, nodding toward the ranch.

"Oh, you've never been out here before?"

"No. Usually when George or Adam need my services they come into town. I imagine they have other errands that day."

"Yes, this is four times the size of what we had back in Texas. Of course, it supports three families, the Larsons, Colters, and Cahills. Then there's Adam's stables and horse training."

"I've heard he is the best in the territory."

"He is. It's one of those things that just came naturally to him. And to Julia, his wife, too."

"Did you miss all of them?"

Mel sighed. "I hadn't realized how much until we crested that last hill."

They arrived at the bottom of the road. Alex pulled the carriage to a stop next to the Andersons' wagon.

"You know how to unhitch and care for the horse?" she asked.

"Not really."

"I'll show you."

She walked over to the horse and began unfastening several leather straps. She glanced at him a few times to make sure he watched.

"You have to think in reverse when you go to hitch it up again."

He chuckled. "Maybe you could show me that later."

"Tomorrow when we leave, I'll show you."

"Tomorrow?"

She glanced up at him. His face turned red.

"Oh, no. I didn't tell you we would stay overnight?" She felt terrible.

He shook his head. "I guess that's why you brought a bag?"

"I'm so sorry. Did you bring anything?"

"No. Even less since you half undressed me."

Her face warmed as he winked at her.

"Don't worry, I won't tell your parents."

Mel cleared her throat and nudged him out of the way as she led the horse to the stable. Then, as her face cooled, she showed him how to brush down the horse. He placed his hand on top of hers and matched her movements. Goodness, he stood so close she could feel the warmth of his body.

"Looks like you've got this." She handed him the brush and stepped back.

"I'd liked it better when I had your help," he teased.

Her face warmed again. She liked the playful version of Alex.

When they finished caring for the horse, she led him toward the doors.

"Mel?"

"Hmm?" She turned to face him.

He placed his hands on her waist as he stood in front of her, blocking the exit. "Would you let me kiss you?"

The air left her lungs and she felt lightheaded. She blinked. Her eyes traveled up the buttons of his shirt, then his beard, then to his eyes.

"I…"

How silly would it be to say she had never been kissed before? Didn't know how?

"Alright," he said, releasing her. He stepped to the side. "You're not ready, yet and that's fine. I'll wait for you, Melissa Larson."

Then he stepped out of the barn and into the bright sunlight. She stood there for a moment from the safety of the barn and watched him watching the activity of the ranch. Though his beard and mustache hid his lips, she could tell he was smiling because his cheeks pushed up closer to his eyes.

She had only met him a week ago. A week. A tumultuous week. Was it only Monday that she disrespected him in court by making an example of him? How had she come to feel so strongly for him so quickly?

"Yes," she said.

His head snapped to the side, and he quirked an eyebrow.

"Yes, you may kiss me."

In two strides, he pulled her into his strong arms and kissed her softly on the lips. His beard brushed against her skin, and it was softer than she thought it would be. She slid her arms around his neck and stood on her tiptoes. As she did, he deepened the kiss. She copied his movements, guessing that was the way to kiss. When he groaned, she pulled away.

He let go of his hold on her waist and took her hand in his.

"I'm sorry. You must think me an idiot," she rushed to explain. "That was my first kiss, and I don't know—"

Alex cocked his head to the side. "That was your first

kiss?"

She slumped her shoulders forward. "It was that bad?"

He snorted. "Mel Larson, you are a woman who excels at everything you do. I quite enjoyed it."

Heat warmed her face. She wasn't sure if it was normal to talk about a kiss after it happened. It all seemed so strange to her. The actual kissing had been delicious.

He kissed her cheek and stepped away.

"Missy!" Adam's voice preceded him as he stepped into the barn. "There you are. We thought we saw you arrive a while ago."

Her face warmed and she looked down at the floor.

"Oh, Alex," Adam said when he noticed him. "Good to see you."

"Adam." The men shook hands.

"I brought Alex with me," Mel said hoping her voice did not betray any of her jumbled feelings. She squared her shoulders. "And call me, Mel. I'm done with the childhood nickname."

"Whatever, Missy. I don't think there's a soul on this ranch that will be doing that. Except maybe him," he said pointing to Alex. "You've kept everyone waiting long enough. Let's go."

Her brother nudged her out into the bright sunlight and escorted her toward the large crowd waiting between the houses on the property. Alex followed behind them.

She smiled. He said she was a good kisser. Guess maybe some things came naturally. Or maybe it was because she was with him. She did not know, but she would have to think about it later.

"Missy!" Sisters, brothers, nieces, nephews, and her parents swarmed her with hug after hug. She rolled her eyes toward Alex any time they used her childhood nickname.

He smiled in return.

Mama hugged Mel as she scolded her. "You didn't say you were bringing a guest. We might have to put him up in the barn."

"Mama," Helen, her youngest sister said, "we are not putting the District Attorney in the barn. Missy and I will share my room. Then he can have her room."

Mel's face warmed. "That sounds like a good idea." She mouthed the word "sorry" to Alex. He winked at her.

"Missy, er Mel." Papa pulled her close for a tight hug. "I saw you in court yesterday."

"You did?"

"You were amazing. Put this feller in his place."

"Alex," George greeted him and shook his hand.

After Alex greeted Papa, he said, "In the end, justice won. That's all that really matters to me."

"Spoken like a politician." Papa slapped him on the back. Then he put his arm around Mel. "What do you say we get this welcome home party started?"

"Where's Bethie?" she asked not seeing her remaining sister.

"Hawk went into town to get her," Mama said.

"They've been courting for a while," Papa said.

"I do hope they will get married soon," Mama said. "They seem so happy together."

Mel kept her thoughts to herself. She was surprised that her parents were fine with a cowboy courting their daughter. When she lived on the ranch, it had been considered taboo. Maybe her parents softened their discipline with child number five, Bethie, and number six, Helen.

"It's still a little early for lunch so why don't you to go say hi to all the cowboys and play some games," Mama said, as she ushered Mel and Alex toward the corral.

As they walked away, Mel overheard her Mama say, "Don't you think he's too old for her, George?"

"Nonsense. Probably about a nine-year age difference. Bethie's man is seven years older than her. Besides…" Papa's voice faded as she was too far away to hear what else he said.

"So your mother thinks I'm too old for you," Alex said.

"And how old are you?"

"Now, you know it's not polite to ask a man his age." He tugged on one of her curls. "I'm thirty-one now. Will be thirty-two in August."

She frowned. He was a little older than she thought.

"And you?" he asked.

"If it is impolite to ask a man his age, then it must be scandalous to ask a woman her age." She nudged him with her shoulder.

"Well, you already kissed me like a woman, so please tell me it was legal."

She laughed. "Twenty-two now. Twenty-three in October."

Nine years. Papa had been right. It was almost like he already checked into that. She would not be surprised. Having four daughters on a ranch made a man cautious and aware of who his daughters were around.

"Oh, good. We're legal then. And I don't have to sleep in the barn tonight. I think this might turn out to be a good day."

"Are you always so good natured?" she asked.

"Do I need to remind you about Monday? In fact, I never did apologize for dressing you down outside the courthouse. I was out of line."

"I've already forgotten about it."

CHAPTER 15

Alex walked with Mel over to the corral. Several cowboys greeted her by name. She greeted them back.

"Missy."

A young man with a beautiful young woman on his arm stood a few feet away. When Mel turned to them, Alex noticed a flash of something on her face. Before he could figure it out, it had passed.

"Hawk. Bethie. How good to see you both! Mama told me the good news."

Bethie pulled her man closer. "I'm glad to hear you say it's good news."

Mel ignored the barb. "Alex, this is Hawk and my second to youngest sister Bethie."

"Pleasure to meet you both," he said as he shook Hawk's hand.

"Hawk was the investigator who uncovered that information I shared with you yesterday afternoon."

Alex nodded.

"I can't thank you enough," Mel said. "Your information saved an innocent man."

Alex noticed her sister tighten her hold on Hawk's arm. He figured either Hawk and Mel were an item at one time or one of them liked the other, though it did not seem like Mel noticed.

"Alex, if you need an investigator for your office, you should hire Hawk. He's very good at tracking and investigating."

"I will keep him in mind." And he would. Given the information he uncovered on the Gutierrez murder, it seemed Hawk had ferreted out the real killer in a short period of time. He could use talent like that.

"Come on, Missy!" Adam called out to them from a game of horseshoes. "I want to see what kind of horseshoe player your friend is."

Alex cringed.

"Do you—"

"No," he whispered. "Never played."

"I can discreetly teach you if you'd like, but we'll have to play on opposing teams. You might get bested by me and Julia."

"My pride can take it."

Julia stood next to her husband Adam while Mel told him to stand next to her. As Julia tossed the first horseshoe at a pole in the ground, Mel explained the game.

"See this line?" She pointed to it with her foot. "You have to stand behind it when you throw the horseshoe. When it's your turn, you want to get the shoe in the pit— that's the rectangle around the stake. Anything outside of the pit doesn't count."

Julia tossed the horseshoe underhanded. It hit the stake.

"A ringer on your first throw!" Adam groaned.

"That's three points for us," Mel said softly so only he could hear.

"Your turn," Julia said.

Adam stood behind the line and threw underhanded. His landed inside the pit but not as close as Julia's was. Julia took another turn. Hers landed closer to the stake than Adam's.

Then he threw and it was on the line of the pit.

"We've got five points. Your team has none," Mel explained.

"None?" Alex asked confused. "You mean we don't get points when we land one in the pit?"

"Only the closest two to the stake count. Sorry." She raised her voice, "Julia, what do you say we let the losing team start this round?"

"Go for it," Julia said.

"You're up. Underhanded and behind the line."

She handed him a horseshoe.

Underhanded and behind the line. "Here goes nothing."

When Alex let go of the shoe, it landed on the edge of the pit but partly outside. "Drat."

"Better luck next time."

As she lined up and started to throw, he said, "Good luck, Missy."

She released it seconds later and it landed short of the pit.

"That's cheating," she said.

His next pitch landed close to the stake but did not touch it. Her second pitch was a ringer.

"Do we at least get a point for mine?"

She laughed. "Yes, but you two are in a big deficit. I'm not sure you can win unless you cheat."

"I don't cheat."

She raised an eyebrow.

He really did enjoy teasing her.

They played a few more rounds until Julia and Mel thoroughly defeated him and Adam. He walked across the court.

"I thought with you being a horse trainer, you would be good at this game."

Adam laughed. "Would you believe me if I told you that

I let my wife win?"

Alex scrutinized him for a second. "No."

Adam sighed. "She is very good at this and most games. So is Missy. In fact, Missy is by far the most competitive Larson around."

"I kinda figured that out on Monday."

Adam laughed. "In court, I'm guessing."

"Yeah."

"Well, it must not have been too bad given you are here at her welcome home party. I was surprised to see she brought anyone with her. She's only been back for a week."

He knew. He saw her that first day in the café. It was hard to believe that had been only a week and a day ago. It seemed like months had gone by.

"Another round?" Adam asked as Thomas Anderson and Will Colter joined them.

"Sure."

"You and Thomas against me and Will?"

"Why, is Will as good as your wife?"

Adam smiled. "He's her big brother. I'll let you draw your own conclusions."

They played the game, but in between throws, Alex searched the crowd for Mel. She stood with one leg propped on the corral talking with her sister Helen.

"She's a force," Adam said.

"That she is."

A whirlwind that came to town and knocked him off his feet. She was so unexpected and amazing. Full of life.

He was glad she invited him to the ranch. She was different here. Fun. Free. All hint of competition or striving faded away. She was just Mel.

And she was headed his way.

"Have you ever seen a pit smoked whole pig before?"

Alex blinked. "Pit smoked whole pig? No."

She grabbed his hand and dragged him over to where Georgie and another man stood. "This is amazing. You have to see this."

"Snake," she said, introducing him to the other man, "this is Alex Glassman. Alex, this is Daniel Raulings, or as we like to call him, Snake. Alex has never seen this before."

"Oh, you're in for a real treat," Snake said.

Snake lifted a plank off the pit. Then he used a shovel to set aside a layer of smoldering coals. Then he lifted some sort of large leaves to reveal a whole pig underneath.

"It's staring at me," he said.

Mel laughed. "Does it bother you?"

"I don't know yet. I'm not used to eating food that is looking at me."

Snake laughed. "Don't worry. By the time I'm done with him, he won't be looking at nobody."

Alex laughed and watched as Georgie and Snake lifted the large pig out of the pit and onto the table. As they pulled meat from the pig, Alex's mouth watered.

"I think I'm over the fact that he's looking at me. Smells delicious. How long ago did you start cooking him?"

"Two days ago."

Alex's eyes went wide. Mel smiled up at him.

"How often do you have pig like this?"

"Rarely. Usually once or twice a year," she said. "Wanna help Mama bring out the rest of the food?"

He agreed and followed her into the Larson's home. It was quaint. A large kitchen and dining room took up one half of the front of the house. A parlor took up the other half. A long hallway was on the other side of the parlor, which probably led to the bedrooms.

She handed him a pan of food. "Set it on the long table

outside. Anywhere will be fine."

She followed him out with something heavy, so he took it from her and set it on the table. Her sisters filed out one by one with more food and plates and silverware. The Colter and Cahill families contributed more of the same.

"How many people live here?" he asked as they all gathered around several long tables.

"Probably around sixty or so when you include all the cowboys. There's several out with the herd today," Mel replied.

He could hardly believe it. It made his childhood plantation look tiny.

George Larson got everyone to quiet down for the blessing. Then he prayed rather eloquently, expressing his gratitude for his daughter coming home and for the food. When he finished, everyone took a seat and began passing food around.

Alex grew quiet. It was obvious both her father and mother loved Mel deeply. Not just her but all their children. It must have been wonderful to grow up in such a loving home.

His father had been anything but loving. He only loved Franklin, his older brother. Alex held back a snort. He was not entirely sure if Solomon Glassman even loved his own wife. As harshly as he spoke to her in front of Alex and his siblings, he often wondered if Father had been as harsh behind closed doors.

He frowned. He vowed he would never treat a woman like that.

Except he had. On Monday. Outside the courthouse. He had been almost as vicious and cruel as his father to Mel.

He sighed. He apologized for it, but it still scared him that such darkness came out of him that day. He had not known it lurked there. He hoped to never act in such a way again.

Mel slid her hand onto his knee. He froze.

"What's wrong?" she asked as she removed her hand.

"Sorry. I was just thinking about how opposite your family is to mine. You are clearly loved by a lot of people."

"You weren't?"

The compassion in her eyes made him love her even more.

"No, I was not."

He took a bite of the pulled pork. It was the most tender, juicy, and flavorful meat he had ever tasted. He pointed at it with his fork. "This is amazing!"

She smiled and his heart lifted. "It is, isn't it?"

CHAPTER 16

Mel smiled as she carried dishes to a large makeshift wash basin. It would take the Larson girls some time to get through all the dishes.

Alex headed off by himself for a while, probably trying to find a quiet place to think. She could imagine it was a different experience for him being around such a large group of people.

"He seems very taken with you," Caroline said as she rolled up her sleeves. "Let me help wash."

Mel scooted over so they could both wash. Helen stood next to Mel and Bethie next to Caroline. Both were ready to receive clean dishes and set them out to dry in the sun.

"Yes, he hasn't taken his eyes off you this whole time. Even now," Helen said.

"Really?" Mel asked.

Helen pointed over towards one of the rockers on Mama's front porch. He nodded when she looked his way.

"Isn't that like our, Missy," Bethie said. Her tone was rather acidic. "Turning every boy's head."

"What's on your mind, Bethie?" she asked. She would not tolerate her sister's passive aggressive comments.

Bethie did not answer.

"Has he kissed you yet?" Caroline asked.

Mel's face turned bright red.

"He has. When?"

Mel cleared her throat. "In the barn when we first got here. It was my first kiss, you know."

"Really?" Helen asked.

"I doubt that," Bethie said. "The way you and Hawk carried on before you left…"

Mel dropped the plate into Helen's hands and turned toward Bethie. "Is that what this is about? Are you worried I've come back to steal your beau away?"

Bethie narrowed her eyes and took a step closer. "Do you really expect me to believe that you and Hawk never kissed? Not once?"

"Believe it. And if you don't believe me, ask him. You should be able to speak about these things if you plan on marrying him."

"Please," Helen said. "Can't we get along?"

"Shut up, Helen. Don't take her side," Bethie said.

"I'm not taking anyone's side. It's just been a really long time since we've all been together. I miss it and I just want us to be friends."

Bethie opened her mouth, but Caroline cut her off.

"Enough. Helen is right. It's been a long time since we've been together. Bethie, you have nothing to worry about from Missy. She's all mushy around Alex and doesn't have eyes for anyone else. Hawk is madly in love with you, and you are with him. You should not be so insecure about that."

Bethie frowned and stomped away.

Mel sighed. "Does she really think Hawk and I were a thing?"

"Guess so," Caroline said.

"We weren't. We were just friends."

"I'm sorry," Helen said. "She's always been jealous of

you. You're smart and beautiful. She thinks she is not as pretty as you."

"As me? Caroline is the fairest of us all."

"Me? Posh. And certainly not after so many pregnancies."

Mel squeezed her hand in the water. "I'm so glad Wade made it."

"Me, too." Caroline's eyes teared up. "I can't bear to lose another child. Three living and three dead. I still mourn every baby I've lost."

Helen hugged Caroline. "I know. I'm so sorry, Linny."

Caroline snorted. "It's been forever since any of you have called me that."

"How do I get you all to stop calling me Missy and call me Mel instead?"

"Oh that?" Caroline said. "It's never gonna happen. Especially since we know how much it bugs you."

Helen and Caroline laughed. Mel looked over to where Bethie stewed.

"Don't worry," Helen said. "She'll come around. She's nervous, you know. They've been courting for eight months, and he still hasn't proposed."

"He's still a cowboy at the ranch?" Mel asked.

"Yes, I think that's part of it," Caroline said. "He doesn't want to take a wife while working for her father as cowboy."

"Maybe I can talk to Alex. He really needs a better investigator at the DA's office. I mentioned it earlier, but I'll let him know Hawk is serious about a new position."

"Oh, Bethie would be so happy. She really wants to marry him," Helen said.

"What about you, little Helen? Anyone caught your eye?" Mel asked.

"She's been too busy helping me out before Wade was born. She only just moved back home a few days ago."

"Oh."

"There is someone," Helen said as she took the next dishes from Mel and Caroline. She set them on the table and came back.

"Spill it," Mel said.

Caroline laughed. "Is that a tactic you learned from Mr. Pittman?"

"No." Mel laughed.

They both stared at Helen who lifted her chin. "I'm not ready to say anything yet."

Mel smiled. She knew Caroline would get an answer by the end of the weekend.

"Caroline," Thomas said, looking at the sky. He had Lily leaned up against his chest. Her head snuggled against his neck. Drew held Thomas's other hand and yawned. "We should get these two home."

"You're not staying?" Mel asked.

"No. There's not enough room and who wants to sleep with a newborn?"

Mel dried her hands on her apron. Then she hugged Caroline and Thomas goodbye.

When Caroline left, Adam's oldest daughter joined them.

"Hi Aunt Missy and Aunt Helen. Do you need some help?"

"Thank you, Catherine," Mel said. "My you've grown up while I was away. How old are you now?"

"Seven."

"Do you go to school in town?" she asked as she handed her a plate. She carried it carefully over to the table and set it down. Then she ran back.

"No. Aunt Mary teaches us at her house."

Helen explained. "Mary Cahill decided there were enough children on this ranch to hold school here. There are her two oldest, Eddie and Bethie. Then most of Will's boys are in school. Then Adam's two oldest and Georgie's oldest. Then Pedro and Rosa have one or two in school. In all I think that comes to ten. Could you imagine trying to get all of them ready to go into town in the morning?"

Mel laughed. "No."

Catherine helped for a few more dishes before she darted off again.

Mel held up her hands. "My fingers look like dried prunes."

"Do you want to switch?" Helen offered. "Now that we're alone, I'll tell you who has my eye."

"Who?"

"Ira. He works for J.W. Harrison & Co., the freighter. Sometimes he's gone for a long time, hauling freight all over the territory. But when he's in town, he sends word. If you don't mind, the next time he comes, can I stay with you? I don't want Caroline to know. You know how she gets about these things."

Mel nodded. "Of course. And I know what you mean about Caroline. I'm sure she's already planning my wedding and I'm not even courting." Yet, she thought.

The sun lowered in the sky as they finished the last dish. Her back ached and her feet hurt. She shivered.

"Too cold for a walk?" Alex asked from behind her.

"Oh, I have a shawl in—"

He held it out for her. "Your mother took it out of your bag. She's the one that suggested the walk."

He nodded toward the house.

Mama waved.

"She would. Have you seen her with Papa? The two of them act like young lovers half the time."

"I have and I think it's adorable. I hope that my future wife treats me like that when I'm old and gray."

Mel shivered, but not from the cold. She placed the shawl around her arms and fell into step beside him.

"Aren't you cold?"

"I am but someone ripped my jacket off me this morning."

"I'm sorry. I just wanted you—"

He placed a finger on her lips. "If I'm going to visit the ranch more often, I will invest in some appropriate attire."

He led her around the lake and once they were on the far side, he continued, "I know we've only just met, Mel. But I already care for you more than I've ever cared for any woman."

"Have there been many?" she asked.

He turned to face her. "Let me finish. If you still want to know later, I'll answer any of your questions about anything."

She nodded. "Continue."

"I think I am falling in love with you already. You came into my life like a whirlwind. I'm like a helpless leaf floating around you, hoping you will carry me with you to a better life."

She sucked in a deep breath. That was positively the most wonderful thing anyone had ever said about her.

"Will you allow me to court you?"

Mel looked into his eyes. He was so vulnerable in that moment. His eyes held such hope.

"I'm not sure. Shouldn't you ask my father first?"

"He said if you accept me, then he will."

Her heart jumped into her throat. "Really? You asked

him already?"

"Yes. I've never been more certain of anything. I want to court you. To woo you. To win your heart."

She hesitated. Would he expect her to give up her independence? She did not know him well enough to gage him. Should she ask? Or could she be patient and learn over the course of a courtship?

"What is it?" he asked.

"I barely know you."

"I know you feel this too. On the porch at my house."

Her faced warmed and she looked at his lips or where she thought they were hidden by his beard and mustache. She remembered wishing he had kissed her then.

"At your house this morning."

Yes, she felt something then too.

"In the barn."

And then.

"So, what is holding you back?"

She took a step back. "I have worked very hard to become an attorney to the fullest extent that the law will allow a woman. I am independent. I work hard. I don't want to give up any of that."

He stepped closer and took her hands.

"I am not asking you to."

"And you won't in the future?"

"No. My goodness, Melissa. Your independence and intelligence are as attractive to me as your beauty."

She liked hearing her full name on his lips.

"Yes," she whispered.

He pulled her close and leaned down as she stood on her tiptoes. She wrapped her arms around his neck as he kissed her with more passion than he had in the barn. His hands roamed over her back. Then he pulled away from her lips and brushed aside some of her hair to expose her neck. He trailed fiery kisses along it. She moaned. She just could not help it. She never felt so amazing before and she liked it.

CHAPTER 17

Alex savored the taste of Mel's lips as he deepened his kiss. She moaned when he kissed her neck, so he moved back to those full maddening lips. She pressed into him and returned the kiss, stirring his blood with every tease and taste.

When she played with his hair, he stopped abruptly. He was acutely aware that they were on her parents' property. He needed to pull back his desire, no matter how badly he wanted her.

He released her and ran a hand down her arm to take her hand in his. She interlaced her fingers with his. He walked them back toward her parents' home.

"This ranch and lake are beautiful," he said. His voice was huskier than he intended. He needed to talk to cool himself down. "It must have been wonderful growing up in such a place."

"I was fifteen when we moved here. Even though I only lived here for four years, this is what I think of when I am afraid and want to feel safe."

He frowned. "Afraid. I have a hard time believing that is something you feel very often."

She shivered and he put his arm around her shoulders.

"Wouldn't you love to paint this?" she asked. "At sunset during the summer monsoons, it is stunning."

He smiled as his heart warmed. "I do think I would like to paint the ranch. Many times, with different lighting."

"I'm sure my parents would not mind if you came out some weekends and did just that. Especially if you bring me with you."

"You wouldn't mind if I brought you and then abandoned you in favor of painting?"

She laughed. "Well, you still need to eat, right? And you don't paint in the evening, do you?"

He would not paint in the evening, but he might draw sketches of her, like when she played horseshoes or chatted with her sisters.

"I suppose you are right."

His heart squeezed. "Are you certain your parents would not look on me unfavorably because I like to paint?" His father had.

"Oh, Alex. No, they would not. My papa is nothing like how you briefly described your father. He is the most loving man I know. He accepts a person for who they are. And painting is a part of you."

He squeezed her to his side as he hoped she was right.

"I would still like to see more of your work sometime. I think you are very talented."

"Thank you."

She sighed. "You are a paradox. A brilliant and intelligent attorney who doles out arguments with logical precision. Yet, your painting expresses a creativity and depth of feeling that you seem to hide from the world."

His stomach tightened. She saw him. The real him. His soul. It was frightening and comforting. He prayed she would take care of his heart and not break it. She held the power to do so, unlike any woman he'd ever known.

"I'm getting pretty cold now. So, we either need to kiss

again or go inside. Your choice," he teased.

"Can I choose both?"

"Hmm. I think I saw a curtain flutter, so unless you want an audience we should probably just head inside."

She sighed. "If we must."

Then she yawned.

"See you're tired. You should sit and catch up with your mother and sisters some more. Just relax for a bit."

He held the door open, and her wild hair brushed against his arm. "Maybe I should have kissed you," he whispered.

She glanced over her shoulder. "Too late now. Everyone is staring at us."

He quirked up one lip in a half smile. "I don't mind if you don't."

Mel hurried into the house.

"There you two are. Care for some supper? George was getting a little hungry, so the girls and I are warming up some leftovers," Maggie said as he stepped into the house.

"I could eat."

"Missy, why don't you help us? Alex, make yourself at home in the parlor."

Alex walked over to stand by the fire. George greeted him.

"How was your walk?" George asked.

Alex smiled. "Very nice."

George laughed. "Don't keep an old man in suspense. Did my independent headstrong daughter say yes?"

Alex nodded.

"Good. Sometimes I worry about her. Maggie and I thought she might avoid falling in love if she thought she would have to choose between her job and love."

"She won't have to choose one over the other with me,"

Alex said.

George rubbed a hand over his short beard. "She's going to struggle to find her way with a job and raising a family. You will have to be patient with her. I do believe she wants both, but there's not many women who have paved the way ahead of her. She will need time to figure it out."

Alex nodded slowly and considered George's advice. He spoke almost as a future father-in-law and not as the father of a young woman courting. Perhaps George understood a few things he did not.

"Maggie and I had a very short courtship. Two months. I'm not sure if our girls even know that. There was an instant connection between us from the very beginning. Almost like we had always known each other even though we had just met. After we married, we had our ups and downs trying to navigate what it means to share life together.

"When the Bible says the two become one, it's talking about more than just the marriage bed. It is two hearts, two souls, and two intellects taking a lifetime to merge together in seamless harmony.

"The more independent and headstrong one or both parties are, the more challenging it can be."

Alex nodded and took George's words to heart. He heard the indirect warning: Mel might be a challenge and he would need to be patient. He also heard the unspoken wisdom: he would need to compromise and examine himself, so he did not become too headstrong and independent.

"Supper is ready," Mel said as she smiled at him. She held out her hand.

He crossed the room and took it, allowing her to lead him to the table. He sat next to her and bowed his head as George Larson prayed. He almost teared up when George thanked God for him visiting the ranch and getting to know the family. In that moment he saw what Mel described earlier—her father was a man who accepted another exactly as he was. That was something Alex had not experienced from his own father.

He thought George might have missed something. Two families become one, not that Alex had much family left. Yet, he would not mind becoming a part of hers.

Alex watched as George asked each of his daughters about their work in town. Then he asked Bethie's beau, Hawk, about the work he did for Virgil Pittman.

"Actually, I've been meaning to talk to you," Alex said to Hawk. "Thank you for digging into the Gutierrez case. The information you provided to Mel will help my office look into the right suspect."

Hawk shifted in his chair. "Glad to be of service."

"From what I've seen in my short tenure at the DA's office, I think we could use someone like you on staff. We don't get many murder trials, thankfully, but we do have plenty of cases where we need an investigator with a keen eye for detail and the determination to find the truth. Is it something you would be interested in?"

Hawk finished chewing some food. He glanced at Bethie. "I think I would like that." Then he looked at George. "Would that be alright with you? I wouldn't want to leave you, Will, and Warren shorthanded. You all have done so much for me."

George chuckled. "We will be just fine. You should go do what God created you to do."

Hawk turned to Alex. "Yes, I would be interested. Let's talk about the details after supper."

Alex agreed.

Do what God created you to do. That was what Alex was doing. That must be what George advised Mel to do. He gained a deeper respect for the man.

CHAPTER 18

After supper Mel's family retired to the parlor, along with Alex and Hawk. The conversation ebbed and flowed, but Mel's mind was distracted. She really wanted to talk to Mama about her courtship with Alex.

At nine o'clock, Alex yawned.

"Let me show you to your room," Mama said as she led Alex back to Mel's old room.

Hawk took the opportunity to head back to the bunkhouse. Bethie retired to her room and Papa retired to his. Only Mel and Helen waited in the parlor for Mama to return.

"He's a good man," Mama said as she took a seat by the fire.

"Mama, how did you know you were ready to marry Papa?" Mel asked.

Helen snickered. "Didn't you just start courting this evening?"

Mel glared at her.

"George and I married very quickly."

Mel's jaw went slack.

Helen gasped. "Really?"

"I think twas two months. George would know for certain. He could tell ya the number of days."

Mel smiled. She loved when a hint of Mama's Irish upbringing sneaked into her tone.

"We instantly felt a connection. He kissed me the very day we met."

That was much faster than Mel thought.

"Sometimes your heart just knows. Though, you need to be careful to discern the difference between attraction and love. With love, you want to get to know him more. You see the man he is deep in his heart. A man's heart is a treasure, ya know."

"But does love include attraction?" she asked.

"Aye, it does. Attraction alone or lust is selfish. It desires to take for itself. It puts pleasure first." Mama fanned her face. "Can't say I ever expected to have such an honest conversation with my daughters. Does what I'm saying make sense?"

Mel nodded. The way Mama described love sounded a lot like what she and Alex were discovering. She wanted to know him more—to watch him paint, to see him grow as a leader at work, to encourage him in his dreams. He sounded like he wanted the same for her.

"I think I understand," Helen said. "I'm glad we talked about this."

Mel sat up straighter. "I thought no one knew?"

"I told Mama tonight as we cleaned up after supper. I think Ira wants to come meet you," she said to Mama, "and ask Papa's permission to court me."

"My goodness! All three of you girls finding love at the same time. My house will be empty before I know it."

Mel heard the sadness in Mama's voice. "Don't worry, Mama. You still have Adam and Georgie's children to spoil."

"Yes, I do. But I will miss each of you girls. You have all grown into such beautiful and amazing women. I'm very proud of you."

"Thank you, Mama," Helen said as she stood and hurried over to hug Mama.

Mel followed and hugged her too. "I love you, Mama."

Mama dabbed at tear in the corner of her eye. "I love you both. Now off to bed with ya."

Mel giggled and took Helen's arm. "Do you think she knows we'll be up all night talking anyway?"

Helen nodded. "I think she knows."

"Listen," Helen whispered. She put an ear to the door of the room Alex was in. "I think he snores."

Mel put her ear to the door. She didn't hear anything. Then the door opened, and she fell against Alex's chest.

"You're evil!" she whispered loudly as Helen ducked into her room.

"Spying on me?" Alex laughed.

"Maybe I was stopping by for a good night kiss."

"No. Not under your father's roof. Off you go now."

"Fine."

Alex started to close the door. "See you in the morning."

Heat warmed her face as she entered Helen's room.

"You are terrible," she scolded her sister who laughed so hard tears gathered in the corner of her eyes.

"I'm just old enough to tease you now. You should have been nice to me growing up."

"Nonsense. Caroline was the evil sister."

Mel pulled her nightgown from her bag and turned her back to Helen while she changed. When she finished, both of them hurried under the covers.

"Do you want me to brush your hair, like we used to as little girls?" Helen asked.

Mel reached down to her bag and handed her the brush. "Good luck."

"I always wished I had beautiful curls like you."

"You did? They are quite difficult to control."

Helen began brushing Mel's hair.

"Tell me about Ira."

"He's the nicest man. He's a few years older than me, not nearly as many years as is between you and Alex or even Bethie and Hawk. He wants to keep working for J.W. Harrison & Co. He said they are talking about opening an office near Camp Verde. If they do, he would like to move us there."

"We would all miss you terribly."

"I would miss you all too. But it's not so far that we couldn't come back to the ranch a few times a year to visit everyone."

"You say that now. Just wait until you have babies. I'm not sure we would see Caroline as much as we do if we didn't go to the same church."

Helen grew quiet.

When she finished brushing Mel's hair, she turned around and Mel brushed hers.

"We were all very surprised to hear you moved back with no warning," Helen said. "I thought if Virgil was going to bring you back here you would have known with plenty of time to write to us."

Mel's hand stilled. Her heart picked up pace as she searched for an excuse that explained her strange behavior. Anything but the truth.

She resumed brushing Helen's hair. "You know me. I am stubborn. Virgil wanted me to come back but he waited to spring it on me so I would not change my mind."

"I see."

Mel refrained from saying more.

"You would tell us if something was wrong, wouldn't

you?"

Mel replied with as much enthusiasm as she could. "Of course."

She hated to lie to her family. But she could not tell them about Calvin Westbrook and his threats. She hadn't even told Alex about that. Maybe she should.

"It's getting late. You know Mama will have us up at dawn to get ready for church," Helen said. "Will you and Alex come back out after church?"

"I doubt it. I'll be ready for an afternoon nap before starting the work week."

Mel dropped her brush back in her bag. She snuggled down under the warm covers as Helen turned down the lamp.

"I'm glad you're home, Mel."

She smiled. She appreciated that her sister used her new nickname.

"Me, too," she whispered as Helen fell asleep.

––––––

"Mel!"

Someone shook her violently.

She sat up with a start, breathing heavily. Alex stood in the doorway of Helen's room which was flooded with the soft glow of lamplight.

"You were screaming," Helen whispered. "And thrashing."

Alex's eyes looked as worried as Helen's.

"What's going on?" Bethie said from the doorway with a shawl wrapped over her shoulders.

"I'm sorry," Mel said. "It sounds like…" She could not breathe.

"She had a nightmare," Helen said.

She grabbed a shawl for herself and wrapped it around her arms. Then she placed Mel's shawl over her shoulders.

"Sit up."

Mel tried to breathe but air would not fill her lungs deep enough. Her hand started to shake. *Please no. Not in front of Alex. Not in front of my family.*

She felt lightheaded and wanted to lay down again.

Alex swooped into the room and lifted her from the bed. He stumbled as he carried her to the dark kitchen. Bethie lit a lamp. Helen poured a glass of water and set it in front of Mel.

She could not stop shaking. She tried to breathe but only managed small puffs of air. Tears streamed down her face.

Three pairs of eyes stared at her.

"Drink some water," Alex said softly.

She tried to pick up the glass, but her hands shook so violently that water sloshed over the sides of the glass.

Alex sat down next to her and wrapped his arms around her. He ran a hand over her hair. "You are alright. You are safe."

Over and over, he said soothing words until her breathing returned to normal.

"What's going on?" Mama asked as she joined them in the kitchen followed closely by Papa.

"She had a nightmare," Bethie said.

"Here," Alex said as he held the glass for her. "Try to drink some water."

Mel put her lips on the edge of the glass and sipped as he tilted it slowly toward her.

"I'm so sorry. I'm so sorry."

Mama sat down next to her. "You've got nothing to be sorry for."

"What… What time is it?" Mel asked.

"Three o'clock," Papa replied.

Mel looked up at them. They all stared at her. Fear. Confusion. Helpless.

The sobs came then. They always did. She could never keep it bottled up for long.

"Has she said anything to you?" Mama asked over her head.

"No," Alex replied.

"Baby girl, tell me what has you in such a state."

"I can't. I can't."

"Melissa Larson, we can't help you if you don't let us," Mama's voice was soft as she placed a hand over hers.

Mel took a deep breath and closed her eyes. There was only one thing to do.

CHAPTER 19

Alex's pulse started to slow down. To say that Mel screamed in her sleep was putting it mildly. He woke to her shrieks of terror. It chilled him to the bone.

As he held her to his side in the kitchen his heart broke. Something horrible had happened to her. His mind imagined many possibilities, but they were too appalling to consider.

Her mother pressed her to tell them what was going on.

"Westbrook is out."

"I don't understand," Maggie said. "Who is Westbrook?"

Alex filed the name away. He would find the case and read the details as soon as possible.

"Calvin Westbrook was a client of mine. He murdered…" She shivered and Alex rubbed his hand over her shawl-covered arm. "He murdered his wife."

Her voice sounded far away and numb, breaking Alex's heart even more.

"He was convicted as he should have been. At the sentencing, when the judge told him he was going to spend the rest of his life in jail, he shoved Virgil and Junior out of the way."

Her voice broke as Alex's heart picked up pace.

"He knocked me to the ground."

His jaw twitched.

"And he choked me until I almost blacked out."

Alex looked around the kitchen. Both of her sisters shed silent tears. George moved to stand behind Mel. He rested both of his hands on her shoulders.

"I can still smell him when I wake up from these nightmares. I feel his spit on my face and his hands around my neck."

Alex would go after Calvin Westbrook. He would make sure that man never laid a finger on her again.

"It took four men to pull him off me."

Maggie gasped.

"He went to prison."

Mel buried her face in his chest, and he held her close.

"He wrote to me in prison. These horrifying letters describing how he would kill me when he got out."

She looked up at him. "It was always 'when' and not 'if'. I just realized that."

Alex kissed her forehead.

"I never told Virgil about the letters."

His stomach tightened. "How long ago was the case?"

"Four years ago. It was my first case."

Maggie looked up to George. George's frown reflected his own.

"Everything was fine for a while. The nightmares came and went, but I handled it."

He was both proud and frustrated with her for trying to carry it all on her own.

"Then he escaped from prison on February twenty-fifth. There was a newspaper announcing his escape waiting for me on my desk when I got out of court. Virgil thinks Westbrook put it there."

Alex closed his eyes trying to control his anger.

"That's... That's why I came home with no warning.

We were afraid he would come after me and carry out his threats."

She sat up straight and looked around the room. "I'm so sorry I ruined the day."

George nodded to Alex, and he slid over to allow the man to comfort his daughter. George pulled her against his broad chest. "Hush now. You did nothing wrong, Melissa. You're safe now."

Alex stood and walked out to the front porch despite the freezing air. Why had Virgil not said something to him? He was the District Attorney. He could have been monitoring the manhunt for Westbrook from afar. He could have read through the case files and been ready to help. All of which were things he would see to as soon as he was back in town.

He took a deep breath as he paced the length of the porch.

"You didn't know, son." It was a statement and not a question. George joined him on the porch. "Not much we can do for those we love when they keep secrets from us."

Alex shook his head. "Virgil knew. He could have said something."

"And what do you suppose he would say? That he brought Missy home to keep her safe. That's a conversation he could have had with me, but not you. It would have killed a part of her to know that her peers, fellow attorneys would look at her differently because of it."

"So, you think that's why she kept it quiet?"

"Positive of it."

Alex rubbed his hand over his beard several times.

"What are you thinking?"

"I'm going to talk to Virgil about it as soon as possible. And I'll reach out to the Marshall's Service to see where they are with the man hunt. I'll also get a copy of the court records so I can be familiar with the trial and case against Westbrook. I will do whatever I can to keep her safe."

"You might start with praying."

Heat warmed Alex's face. George was right. It was the place to start.

"Come back inside. Try to get more sleep."

When Alex and George came back in the house, Mel sat on a sofa in the parlor rocking back and forth. Maggie sat with her. Her sisters must have returned to bed.

George took a seat on the other side of Mel. Then he bowed his head as he and Maggie prayed over their daughter.

Alex turned and walked down the hall back to Mel's old room. He closed the door behind him. As he took off his pants and laid in bed again, his mind raced. He would do anything to keep Mel safe.

CHAPTER 20

The next morning, Mel woke with a splitting headache. Helen was already up and gone from the room. She went over to the wash basin and washed up. Then she donned the lavender dress she brought for church.

When she opened the door and stepped into the hallway, the smell of bacon greeted her. The clock on the wall chimed ten o'clock. They missed church and it was her fault.

She trudged into the kitchen and found her parents, sisters, and Alex eating.

"I'm sorry."

Mama came over and hugged her. "There is nothing to be sorry for. Have a seat. We just sat down."

Mel slid into the chair across from Alex. She could not look him in the eye. She remembered most of what happened last night. He must think her a silly weak fool.

Helen dished up a plate and set it in front of Mel.

She took a fork and moved the food around on her plate.

"Are you feeling alright?" Helen asked.

"I have a headache."

Helen stood and went to the stove, most likely to make some willow bark tea.

She felt a foot nudge hers. She looked up.

Alex smiled at her.

She looked down at her plate as tears silently trailed down her cheeks. "Excuse me," she said before she got up and ran out the door.

Mel plopped down in one of the rocking chairs on the porch and bawled. She wished she could saddle a horse and run back to town instead of having to face her family.

Helen brought her the willow bark tea and sat down next to her. She rubbed her back and handed her the tea.

Mel wiped the tears from her face and sipped the tea.

"You should not be so hard on yourself," Helen said softly. "What you are going through is no small thing."

She took another sip. Helen was the sister that seemed the most aware of someone else's feelings. She always spoke calmly. Her voice and demeanor were very comforting.

"No one judges you, you know."

"I'm sure Alex would love to run for the hills and take back his request to court me." She sipped more tea.

"He was up pretty early sitting on the floor outside of our room."

"Why?"

"He was praying for you and waiting for you."

Mel finished off the tea. Her heart warmed some, but she still felt very embarrassed about everything.

"He wanted to bring you the tea even now. He's very worried about you."

"So, he doesn't want to run back to town and forget that he ever met me?"

"Quite the opposite. He's a good man, Missy. I mean Mel. You can rely on him, especially when you get back home."

Mel handed her the mug. "I suppose Adam and Georgie know."

"Papa told them just enough to explain why we were

not going to make it to church today."

Helen gave her a long hug.

"Come eat something."

Mel stood and followed Helen back inside.

She took the same seat and tried to eat.

"If you'll excuse me," Alex said, "I'll go get the carriage ready. I'm sure you are ready to go home."

She looked up at him. "And you remember how to harness the horse?"

Alex snorted. "No, not really. Thanks for telling my secret."

"I'll help," Papa said.

The two men left.

Mel let out a long breath.

"Melissa," Mama said. "We are here for you if you need us. George and I will pray for you like we always do. You should not feel bad about what happened. You have been carrying a very heavy burden on your own for too long."

"That's right," Bethie said. "If you ever just want to talk, I'm over at the Harrison's home. And of course, you know Caroline is there for you too."

"Do you want me to stay with you for a while?" Helen asked.

"No. I'll be fine. Really."

"If you change your mind…"

Mel ate a few bites of food while her sisters cleaned up the rest of the dishes. By the time they were almost done, she was ready to hand over her half-eaten meal.

She went down the hall to Helen's room and packed up her things. When she returned to the parlor, Alex waited for her.

"Ready?"

She nodded. Then she said her goodbyes to her family.

When she stepped out of the house her headache finally faded. Alex took her bag and set it in the carriage. She climbed in and sighed. He climbed in next to her and waved to her family as he drove up the hill.

"I'm so sorry. You must think I'm—"

"The bravest woman I know."

She glanced up at him.

"Mel, I'm the one who is sorry. I'm sorry you have been carrying this around for so long. How often do you have the nightmares?"

She cleared her throat. "Fairly often."

He put an arm around her shoulders, and she scooted closer, wrapping her arms around his middle.

"Once a week?"

Silence.

"Twice a week?"

"They come and go. Less often when there are no triggers. More often when there are."

He rubbed a hand up and down her arm.

Tears welled up again and she turned her face into his chest.

"Let it out," he whispered as he rubbed her back.

They were more than halfway back to town by the time she got her crying under control.

"I'd offer you a handkerchief, but it might be one of the pieces of my wardrobe that you stole."

She snorted. "You did look very handsome all gussied up."

He laughed. "Gussied up, huh? You better believe I'm going shopping after work tomorrow to get some denim and maybe a cotton shirt like your father was wearing."

"I bet you'll look handsome in that, too."

"Should I get a cowboy hat? I feel like that might be trying too hard."

"Whatever makes you happy."

He pulled the carriage to a stop in front of her house. Then he grabbed her valise and came around to help her down.

"Remember, I have a few things you need to return."

"Come on in," she said as she unlocked the door. "You can toss that on the sofa."

She picked up his things. "One neck scarf. One jacket. A bowler hat. And two very special cuff links."

"Thank you, my sweet Mel."

She smiled up at him.

He made no move to leave.

"I had a really great weekend, despite our early morning moment," he said.

She looked down at the floor. Her smile faded and she backed away. Her hands started shaking. "What. Is. That."

Her throat constricted.

Alex leaned down and picked up the envelope with her name scrawled on it.

"Mel, sit down."

She couldn't breathe.

"It's." A gulp for air. "Him."

Alex frowned and opened the envelope. He scanned the page, and his face went white.

CHAPTER 21

Alex set his things down and picked up the envelope. He tore it open and read.

His chest squeezed as he read the description of what Westbrook wanted to do to Mel. It was graphic and horrifyingly detailed. He folded it up and put it in his jacket pocket to keep as evidence.

Then he took a deep breath. Mel needed him to be calm and to help her. He would vent his anger later.

"Mel, look at me."

She shook and had trouble breathing. Her gaze remained unfocused.

He kneeled on the floor in front of her and took her hands. "Mel, look at me."

Her eyes were wide with terror, like a hunted animal with its foot caught in a trap.

"Missy!"

She looked at him then.

"Deep breath. You're safe."

She took a shaky breath.

"Deep breath."

The next one looked deeper to him.

He sat there with her for several minutes until the fear passed. Then he stood slowly. He shook off the numbness in his feet.

"I need to lay down," she said.

Alex hesitated for a moment. She needed to go to her bed.

She stood and started to collapse. He scooped her up in his arms and carried her upstairs. Propriety be cursed. He figured her room was the large one, so headed for it. Then he laid her down on her bed. She was out cold.

His heart raced. He needed to leave her to get the sheriff over to investigate. But he didn't want her to wake up to an empty home and be terrified all over again.

After several minutes, he laid a shawl over her and went back downstairs. He found her key and then locked the door behind him. Then he hurried towards the sheriff's office.

Alex passed Pittman and Associates along the way and wondered if he should talk to Virgil. He would not be in the office since it was still Sunday, but he might know more.

Once he arrived at the sheriff's office, he explained the situation and the two of them headed over to Virgil's home.

"What's going on?" Virgil asked as he opened the door.

"I brought Mel home from the ranch to find this slid under her door," Alex said, handing him the letter from Westbrook. "We should talk as we walk back over there. We shouldn't leave her alone."

Virgil read the letter on the way back to Mel's. "We had some mail from the Tucson office yesterday. I asked an associate to drop this off at her house."

"You need to screen the mail from your Tucson office," Alex growled. "She didn't read this one, but by her reaction she could guess what it said."

"What do you mean?"

"She recognized his handwriting."

"How?" Virgil asked.

Alex slowed as they approached Mel's front porch. "Because she's gotten many letters from him over the years."

All the color drained from Virgil's face. "Like this one?"

"Don't know for certain, but I imagine they are."

"She never said."

Alex unlocked the door and let them inside. "She was sleeping when I left. Let me go check on her."

He took the stairs two at a time. When he peeked into her room she was still sleeping exactly as he left her. He joined the other men in her parlor.

"Do you know where this Westbrook fellow is?" the sheriff asked.

"He broke out of jail," Virgil replied. "That's why Mel moved here. We figured he didn't know she has family here. We thought she would be safe."

"We need to check with the Marshall's Service to find out the status of the manhunt," Alex suggested.

"Can I look around?" the sheriff asked.

Alex nodded.

"How do you know she received other letters?" Virgil asked.

"I went out with her to her family's place this weekend. She had a horrible nightmare this morning and told her family and me a little about Westbrook."

"And she said he sent her letters?"

"Yes."

Alex paced the length of the room. He was furious with Virgil for being so clueless.

"Who... Who is there?" Mel's voice came from the top of the stairs.

"It's me," he said moving to where she could see him. "I've got Virgil and the sheriff here too."

She tentatively took one step down. Then another.

He gave her an encouraging smile.

When she reached the first floor, he helped her over to the velvet sofa. "Would you like some water?"

She nodded.

He went into the kitchen and found a glass then pumped water from the pump in the kitchen sink.

"Why didn't you tell me there were letters?" Virgil asked.

Alex frowned. That was not the time to question her.

"Here," he said as he handed her the glass. Then he sat next to her on the sofa and put his arm around her shoulders.

The sheriff joined them. "I don't see any signs of forced entry. No signs of anyone in the yard either."

"I really think it was the envelope that came in yesterday's mail to the office," Virgil said.

"So, we don't think Westbrook is in town?" Alex asked.

"No."

Mel let out a shaky breath.

"If I had known he was writing to you, I would have opened it first," Virgil said. "I will from now on."

"Excuse me a minute," she said. She went upstairs and moved a few things around in the room above them. Then she returned with a large stack of folders.

"What is this?" Alex asked, taking the stack from her.

"My case files and all the letters he's sent me."

She plopped down on the sofa again.

Alex flipped through the first folder. It was full of letters. There was a second and third. The last file was the case paperwork.

His jaw twitched. There had to be at least thirty letters there. He read the first one. It was equally disturbing as the one they discovered today.

He looked over at Virgil and handed him the stack. Virgil's face when white as he scanned a few letters.

"Mel, if you had told me, I could have put a stop to this," Virgil said.

"I handled it, Virgil. Those letters are just from the first year. After I spoke with the warden, the letters stopped."

"Until now," Alex said.

"Yes. He either dropped it off at the Tucson office or mailed it there," she said.

The sheriff took a few more notes and then excused himself, with a promise to find out the status of the manhunt.

Virgil stood. "Would you like us to take you to your sister's house? Or back to your parents?"

"No. I don't want anyone else put in danger because I'm with them."

Alex stepped out onto the porch with Virgil. "I don't feel right leaving her alone. Can you stay with her while I go home and change?"

"Alright."

Alex grabbed his things from inside. Then he took the carriage back to Thomas's livery before he hurried home. He washed up as quickly as he could. Then he changed into one of his more casual suits. He grabbed his briefcase from his den and a few other things, then he let Zhao, his servant, know he would not be back until the next day sometime.

Then Alex hurried back to Mel's house. He didn't give a fig if it was improper for him to stay in her home overnight. He would not leave her alone after such a scare.

He stopped by Isabel's to order some food to go. He hoped she liked roast beef.

When he arrived back at Mel's, Virgil greeted him and then left. Mel sat on the sofa gazing into the fire.

"Brought some food," he said as he set it out on the table. He found her coffee and made a pot. "Will you sit with me and try to eat?"

Mel stood and sat down at the table. He prayed for their meal. Mel took a small bite of the sandwich and half-smiled.

"Roast beef. Papa would be proud."

"Oh?"

"That's Colter & Larson beef you're eating."

"It's delicious."

"This isn't mayonnaise on here. What is it?"

"Horseradish."

She chewed slowly. "I like it. It's got more zip to it."

Mel ate half her sandwich and pushed the rest away. She let out a long breath. "I feel like I've lived a month in the last two days."

Alex reached over and squeezed her hand. "I know what you mean."

"Would you mind terribly if I went upstairs and laid down? I have an awful headache."

"Go ahead. I want to read through these papers. I'll be right here if you need anything."

She stood and kissed him on the cheek before she went upstairs.

CHAPTER 22

Alex cleaned up the food and stored the rest of Mel's sandwich in the kitchen. Then he spread the case files across the table. He lit a lamp as the sun set and stoked the fire.

He read several of the letters Westbrook sent to Mel. Each one was graphic. He described how he would kill her. What weapon he would choose. How he would catch her when her guard was down. How many times he would stab her. The details were too vivid. No wonder she had nightmares about the man.

Alex set the letters aside. He picked up the transcript from the court case and read it. The case went on for two weeks. The DA in Tucson presented very clear evidence that Westbrook brutally murdered his wife. He stabbed her sixty-seven times before dismembering her body. His two small children were in the house, though it was unclear if they had seen or heard anything.

Setting the paper down, he wiped a hand over his eyes. If he had been the DA, he would have done his best to keep the children out of the case. It looks like that was the same approach the Tucson DA took.

When the sheriff searched Westbrook's home, they found his bloody clothes and the murder weapon. And the two children crying. It was weeks later before they discovered the body, only after Westbrook made a deal to take the death penalty off the table.

Alex read through page after page detailing the whole morbid scene in the house, what he had done to his wife's body, what he had written on the wall using her blood. Some of it was so gory, Alex's stomach churned.

He stood and walked over to the fireplace. Mel listened to every one of those details and had to mount a defense for the indefensible. His respect for her grew tenfold.

He poured himself another cup of coffee, then read the defense's case. Westbrook swore up and down he was being framed. Mel produced a few men that testified that Westbrook was at a bar with them during the time of the murder, but the timeline was very weak. It overlapped with only part of the time the coroner thought the murder occurred. It was clear that Westbrook could have come home after he left the bar and still committed the violent act.

Alex sighed. If Westbrook treated his own wife so brutally, then the threats he made against Mel were real. If he ever found her alone, Alex was certain the man would do as he threatened.

He needed to do something, but he did not know what he could do.

He read through the rest of the case until the clock read midnight. He was tired. He tidied up the paperwork and placed it on the corner of the table. Then he took the lamp and headed upstairs.

When he entered Mel's room, he found her in her nightgown snuggled under the covers. She looked so peaceful with her long red curls cascading down the sides of her face and neck. She laid on her right side toward the edge of the bed.

It was probably a terrible idea, but he went around to the far side of the bed, turned down the lamp and climbed on top of the covers. He scooted close to her and placed his arm around her waist. He took a deep breath and caught the scent of juniper from her hair. Then he closed his eyes.

Sometime later, he woke up. Dawn streaked blue-gray shadows across the sky. Alex slid from the bed, taking the lamp with him, and went back downstairs.

He felt a small amount of guilt for cuddling with Mel uninvited. It was one practical thing he could do to provide her some comfort.

He dumped out the coffee from the night before and brewed a fresh pot. Then he looked through her cupboards. She had no food. He shook his head. She must have been eating all her meals at the restaurants in town. At least she had coffee.

"Alex," her voice was surprised.

She held a shawl over her nightgown. Her hair looked radiant in the low light. His eyes roamed from her head to her feet. Her ankles and feet were bare and small. Her toes were very cute.

"What are you doing here?"

He cleared his throat. "I never left."

She came closer. "Why?"

He closed the distance between them and placed his hands on her waist. "I couldn't leave."

Mel lifted her gaze to his. She searched his eyes.

He moved his hands to her back pulling her closer. Then lowered his lips to hers. Her shawl fell to the floor as she kissed him back and let her hands roam over his back. His hands explored her back but found their way to her breast. The nightgown was so thin. He could feel its suppleness underneath his touch. She moaned and he deepened the kiss, instead of pulling away. Common sense left him, and he trailed kisses down her neck as his hands freely explored her body. He moved back to her lips again, kissing her with unrestrained passion.

She slid her hands to his chest and pushed him away, breathing heavily.

"You should leave," she said as she retrieved her shawl from the floor.

He tried to slow his breathing. He wanted her so badly it hurt. He took a step back.

"Alex," she said as she walked to the coat rack and retrieved his jacket. "You need to go."

He picked up his briefcase and other things. Then he took his jacket from her hands.

As he started to open the door, she touched his arm. "Thank you for being here. Would you take me out for dinner tonight? I'd like to talk."

His pulse still beat rapidly. He nodded.

"Come by the office around six."

He walked out the door and waited until he heard the lock behind him. Then he hurried down the street toward home as the town woke for the morning. He hoped he didn't ruin his relationship with Mel. It had been foolish to kiss her like that.

———

Mel leaned against the door after Alex left, still reeling from his kiss. He awakened a desire in her that she had no idea existed. Her body did not want her to stop. She wanted to fully explore her feelings through to their natural end.

Thankfully, her logic woke before she did anything she regretted. She wanted to save herself for her wedding night and she knew she had to kick him out in order to preserve herself.

What he did not know was that she woke up sometime after he came to her room last night to find his arm around her. She liked his warmth next to her and the security of his hold. It was the most peaceful she had slept in years.

It was also dangerous. It put both of them in a state of mind to be freer than they should have been.

She swallowed hard and entered the kitchen. She poured some coffee. Then she sat down at the table to collect her wits.

Mel needed to set some ground rules with Alex that evening. She was not angry with him, but she did want to make sure they did not cross a line she was not willing to cross until marriage. The spark between them seemed to grow to a full-on flame in a short period of time. If she wanted the opportunity to get to know him better through their courtship, they would need to severely limit their alone time. More of their interactions needed to be in public or with friends and family around.

She would talk it over with him that evening. Hopefully, he would agree. And hopefully no one had seen him leave her house that morning. She would hate for him to jeopardize his job.

After she finished her coffee, she readied herself for her day. She chose her burgundy dress. She brushed out her hair and pinned back the sides. Then she donned her black hat, picked up her satchel, and headed out the door, locking it behind her.

She stopped at Isabel's for an egg sandwich before walking to the office. When she arrived several associates and Virgil already started their day.

"Mel, a word," Virgil said when he saw she was there.

"What is it?"

He closed the door to his office. "Have a seat."

She did.

"I'm sorry about the envelope. I did not know. If I had, I would never have sent it over to your house."

"All is forgiven."

"I've had word from the sheriff. It sounds like the Marshall's Service is still centering the manhunt around Tucson and Tombstone. They believe Westbrook is still in southern Arizona."

She nodded.

"So, you should be safe."

"Does Alex know?" she asked.

"I don't know. I imagine he'll check in with the sheriff. He seemed very protective of you yesterday."

Heat warmed her cheeks. "We are courting now."

"That was fast."

She laughed. "He came out to the ranch with me this weekend. We have a strong connection and Papa gave his permission, so there you have it."

"Aren't you glad you smoothed things over with him?"

She smiled. "Yes, I am."

"One last thing, I've got a water rights case for you. I'm hoping we can settle this out of court. Maybe attorney to attorney or, worst case, arbitration."

He handed her the file before he opened the office door. She walked down the hall to the library and set her things down. Then she ate her cold egg sandwich as she started reviewing the case. Work was the perfect antidote to the anxiety running just below the surface.

CHAPTER 23

Alex glanced at the clock. Five twenty. He would leave soon to pick up Mel for dinner.

He had been distracted all day. Frustrated, he stroked his beard. He should have been more self-controlled that morning. He loved her but he risked it all by crossing a few lines he knew he should not have, especially so soon.

They had been courting two days. Two very long days that turned into two very long nights. He hated himself for how much he liked cuddling with her last night. It was all he could think about. Then when she came downstairs in her nightgown. It was too much.

Being near her helped heal a part of him that still felt wounded and unloved. Even as she kicked him out of her house, she did so with kindness and an invitation to still see him. She was a far better person than him.

Harrold stuck his head in the open doorway. "We're closing up for the night. You'll be the last out."

Alex nodded before he left.

Harrold had seen him that morning. Not leaving Mel's home but walking from town back to his home. He asked about it, but Alex managed to evade the question. For some reason, the way Harrold persisted in asking questions made him edgy.

He frowned and glanced at the clock again. Five thirty.

Alex pushed back from his desk. He would be early, but he could not wait any longer. He locked up the building and headed over to Pittman and Associates.

He tapped his walking stick lightly against the ground with each step. George said he should not forget to pray. Yet in the last day, he should have prayed but did not. He quickly said a prayer asking for wisdom in how to lead in his relationship with Mel and how to honor her. He asked for forgiveness for crossing some lines.

Arriving at Pittman's office, he opened the door. A light shone in the library and in Virgil's office.

"Hello!" he called out.

"Back here!" Mel answered.

He joined her in the library. Virgil stood across the table from her reading over some of her notes before handing them back.

"I think this might work, but you might want to pick his brain about this one," Virgil said pointing a thumb over his shoulder at Alex. Then he turned to greet him.

"Did the sheriff stop by?" Virgil asked.

"Yes. He said that they are confident Westbrook…" Alex's eyes darted to Mel. She stiffened. "He's not in this area."

"He said the same to us."

Mel set down her papers and rubbed her eyes.

"Ready?" Alex asked her.

She took a sip of water. "Let me wash this. I'll be right back."

He nodded but she did not look at him. His heart sunk. Maybe she was going to break off the relationship with him.

Virgil slapped him on the back.

"Don't look so worried. She's been staring at the clock all day waiting for you."

When Mel returned, she gathered her papers and put them in her satchel. Then she smiled at him, and he breathed a little easier.

"Where are we going?"

"I thought we'd venture out to another restaurant. Show you more than just Isabel's."

She smiled and took his arm.

He led her to the street and to one of the earliest restaurants in town, Osborn's. "If you're feeling adventurous, they have elk on the menu."

"Elk? We occasionally had elk when Georgie went hunting, but it has been ages. Though, I think I am more in the mood for some roast chicken. Just don't tell Papa."

He laughed and let some of his anxiety roll off his shoulders. He stopped a few feet before the restaurant entrance. Taking off his hat, he faced her.

"I want to apologize for this morning. I'm sorry I lost control. The last thing I wanted to do was put you in a compromising situation. Yet, that is what I did. I'm so sorry."

She reached up and placed a hand on his cheek. "I'm sorry too. I knew you were still there. I could have dressed properly before joining you."

He smirked. "I'm not sure that would have made much difference."

She laughed. She took his hat and placed it back on his head. Then she tugged on his arm moving them forward toward the restaurant.

"I think it's safe to say that we both feel very strongly for each other."

He wanted to say that he loved her, already. He knew he never wanted to let her go. That was part of what made it so hard that morning.

"If this, us," she said, "is headed where I suspect both of us want it to, we will have plenty of time for exploring our attraction in the future. For now, I think we would be wise to slow down."

He nodded and remained silent until the server sat them at a table. "It sounds like you may have more to say on the topic?"

"I don't know if it is because we've spent the last forty-eight hours together or because I opened up about my nightmares or because you took such good care of me when I was frightened beyond words. I feel like we've both grown closer together significantly faster than I would have expected."

He took her hand and rubbed his thumb across her knuckles. "I feel it too."

She laughed. "Yes, I figured that out."

The server came back to take their order. When the server left, Mel continued. "I think over the coming months we should limit how often we are alone together. We can spend more time out in public, like tonight, or with friends and family. With Hawk in town now, we can chaperone them as much as they would be chaperoning us. If Ira is in town, I can invite Helen to stay with me, and the six of us could dine together at my house."

"Or at mine. Zhao is a very good cook and I have a large dining room."

"Yes, that would work. Maybe we could invite Caroline and Thomas sometimes. They could probably use a break from their rowdy children."

"I can also invite my sister and nephew, and her husband when he is in town. She is good friends with Caroline."

"We could play cards or charades or other parlor games." Her eyes lit with excitement. "I think it would be as good for us as it would be for my sisters and their men."

She looked away for a moment. "Especially since when Ira marries Helen, he is going to move them away. I know I just got back to town, but I thought my family would remain here. I'm sad that they will be moving."

Alex smiled. "I like your plan. Let me know when and I will make my house open. If there is a menu that you would like served on any occasion, let me know and I'll make sure Zhao prepares it."

She rubbed her eyes and frowned. The server set their plates in front of them.

"What is it?" he asked.

"I have a headache and my eyes are tired."

He waved the server over. "Do you have any willow bark tea?"

The server nodded and brought some right away.

"This afternoon, my eyes blurred a lot. I don't know if I'm just tired or anxious."

"Hopefully the tea will help," he said as the server set it on the table.

Mel sipped the tea between bites of her chicken. "I still would like to see more of your artwork."

Alex suddenly felt nervous. She was asking him for his soul on canvas. That felt like the opposite of taking things slower. He stalled. "I don't know. I'm not sure I want to parade that before your family."

"What about your sister? Have you shown her? I'll bet she would like to see it."

"She doesn't know."

"Promise me, some day you will show me?"

"I promise. When I'm ready."

He chewed a bite of the most tender steak he'd ever eaten. "This Colter & Larson beef?"

"I imagine so. I think the Osborn's were one of Will's original customers."

"Good. I wouldn't want George to be mad at me."

She finished off the willow bark tea. "I think this helped."

"So, I couldn't help noticing you don't have any food in your house. Is that intentional?"

Rosy streaks bloomed on her cheeks. "I just haven't managed to get to the store yet. I probably should have before we went out to the ranch. Though, I really like Isabel's food. This is good too."

He set down his silverware as he finished his food. "If we get married—"

"If or when, counselor?" She raised an eyebrow.

"Hmm. When we get married, I'm guessing you want to keep working, right?"

"Absolutely. For as long as I'm able."

He sighed. "How will that work, if I am District Attorney and you work for Pittman?"

"I imagine I would need to recuse myself from trial if I need to go up against you. Or your ADA would need to handle the case. I suppose it may come down to whatever a judge says."

"I'm hoping we don't end up prosecuting very many of your clients." He wondered though how long he might remain a district attorney. Since meeting Mel, the whole job seemed far less appealing than when he first started. He hated the idea of being on opposing sides of a case. It would be difficult not to talk to her about a case, even as they were courting, much less as husband and wife.

Husband and wife. They danced around the topic and spoke in generalities, but it was what he wanted. More than his job. More than anything else. He wanted a lifetime with

DESERT MANNA BOOK 3

Mel by his side.

"So, you would want to keep Zhao on to continue cooking and cleaning?"

"Would that be my decision?" she asked.

"It would be our decision." He smiled. "But I would fully support what you want."

"Yes. I don't really have time to do much of that now for myself, so we would need the help."

"What about children?" he asked. "Would you want to hire a nanny to help?"

Her cheeks tinged pink again. "I suppose we would need to since we would both be working."

A small part of him hoped she would want to take care of them. But he grew up with a nanny and his mother surely loved him. Perhaps Mel would be able to as well.

They ordered some dessert and talked for another hour before he suggested that he ought to walk her home.

When he led her to her door, he asked, "Do you want me to wait out here for a few minutes? Do you feel safe?"

"I'm fine, Alex. Thank you though."

He gave her a quick gentle kiss on the lips and walked down the porch stairs. He waited from there until she locked the door and lit a lamp. She waved to him from the window before he turned and headed home, smiling all the way.

CHAPTER 24

Mel leaned back in the chair in the library. It was Friday around one o'clock in the afternoon. She rubbed her eyes. Her head pounded yet again.

"Another headache?" Alex asked from the doorway.

She nodded. "Every day now. My eyes are tired."

He frowned and took a seat across from her. "When is the last time you took a break?"

"You're funny. I am getting nowhere with this water rights thing. I need to figure it out." She rubbed her temples and begged the throbbing to stop.

"Have you had lunch?" he asked.

She shook her head.

"Come on, let's go to Isabel's."

He stood and reached for her hand. She put her hand in his and let him escort her to the café.

When they were seated, her eyes started to water. She retrieved her handkerchief and dabbed at them.

"That happy to see me?" Alex teased.

"Well, it has been a few days. I was starting to forget that someone was courting me."

When the server came over, he asked for a willow bark tea for Mel. Then they both ordered sandwiches.

"You should go to the doctor for these headaches. I'm worried about you," he said. He squeezed her hand then released it.

She frowned and sipped on the willow bark tea.

"I'll go with you if you'd like."

"I'm quite capable of going on my own if I choose to."

He raised his hands in defense.

Their food arrived. She nibbled on her turkey sandwich, wishing she had ordered the roast beef.

"Want to split it?" he asked.

"No."

"Are you sure? You've been looking at my sandwich like you might tear it out of my hand."

She snorted. "Fine. Let's share."

She traded him half her turkey for half his roast beef.

"Not bad," he said as he tasted a bite. "I haven't ordered this before."

Mel coughed. She waved a hand in front of her mouth.

"Oh, I forgot to remind you I get extra horseradish. You might want to scrape some of it off."

As she did so, he asked, "What's so peculiar about your water rights case?"

Her shoulders drooped. "It's one of those gray areas. When our client bought some land, the contract did not specify if the water rights came with the land or not. Most of the contracts I've seen will specify one way or the other. I'm just not sure if my client has a leg to stand on if we sue for the rights."

Alex rubbed his fingers over his beard. "That is a tough one. You could take the former owner to court and see where the judge lands. Or you could try to renegotiate with the former owner."

"The former owner is now his neighbor. He sold only part of his land. He has not put up a stink about the new owner trying to drill for a well, but my client is worried that the former owner will sue him."

"Have you tried filing a claim for water rights for the parcel to see what happens?" Alex asked.

A sharp headache hit her, and she closed her eyes for a few seconds. "No."

"Mel, will you please go to the doctor."

"I'll be fine."

"You're not fine. You look like someone beat you with a walking stick."

She opened her eyes.

Alex motioned to the server and requested that she box up their lunches. When she finished, he paid for the meal. Then he carried the boxes and grabbed Mel's hand.

"What are you doing?" she whined.

"Taking you to the doctor."

She let him drag her down the boardwalk to the doctor's office which was thankfully empty. He was able to see her right away.

"I'll wait out here. Make sure you don't run away," Alex teased.

The doctor asked her about her symptoms. Blurry eyes. Watery eyes. Headaches.

"Read this," he asked as he handed her a book.

She squinted and shook her head.

Then he dug around in a drawer and pulled out a pair of spectacles. "Now try."

The words looked much clearer on the page. She looked up in surprise. "How?"

"Do you read a lot?"

"Yes."

"Try these for a few days. If they work for you, then keep them. I can order stronger ones or ones with different strengths for each eye, if need be. Just use them when you read."

"You know Alex is not going to let me live this down."

The doctor laughed and took her payment. Then he escorted her back to the lobby.

Alex greeted her with a raised eyebrow.

She held up the spectacles. "For when I read."

"See. Aren't you glad you listened to me?"

"Fine. I need to go back to the office now."

He walked her there and sat down in the library. He handed her the rest of her sandwich. "You should eat."

"My you are bossy today, aren't you?"

He opened his box and took a big bite of the turkey sandwich. "I get that way when I'm hungry."

She perched the spectacles on her nose and read over her notes. "I guess this is better."

Then she reached for her sandwich and ate a bite.

"They make you look smarter."

She glanced up over the rim.

"Or angrier."

She rolled her eyes.

He winked at her and finished his sandwich.

"Do we have plans for the weekend?" he asked.

"I'm sorry. I hadn't thought about it. I'm sure Bethie and Hawk would be up for dinner tonight or tomorrow."

"Let's say tomorrow. I can stop by the Harrison's on my way home."

She locked her gaze with his. "I heard an interesting rumor the other day."

"Oh?"

"That you and Mrs. Harrison courted for some time before it ended. Then she married Mr. Harrison rather quickly afterward."

Alex frowned.

So, it was true. She wondered when she first heard about it. He never mentioned any previous relationships.

"We didn't love each other. She called me out on it and decided to break it off."

"Were you sad about that?"

He brushed some crumbs off the table. "I was for a while. Even a little jealous when she met Joshua and they married. He and I are friends now. They were destined to be together."

Alex's eyes connected with hers. "She was right. We were not in love. Not even a little. I'm sure she would be thrilled to hear that you and I are."

Mel's heart raced. "In love?"

He smiled. "You love me, Mel Larson. You have from the first moment you met me."

"Well, maybe not the first moment. Maybe more like on your porch when you caught me."

He laughed. "Fine. I'll let you believe that."

"And you?"

His smile faded. "I think I fell in love with you at Isabel's."

"When we had dinner? I was so rude to you for the first half of that meal."

"You were, but I mean when you had lunch with your parents. I was there. I had lunch with my sister, and she gave me no end of grief for staring at you."

"I think I remember that. I was laughing at a story Papa told and I looked over at you to find you staring at me. I guess I hadn't made the connection that it was you."

"Of course, then I hated you that first day of court. You were brilliant and amazing, and you called me out for my assumptions. I loved you and hated you for it."

"Yet, you asked to court me anyway." She smiled.

"I did." He pushed back from the table. "I need to get back to the office. I'll see you tomorrow night at six?"

"Yes. Send word if Bethie and Hawk can't make it."

"Don't you worry, I will find someone to come eat food with us. I miss you."

Her heart warmed at his words and the look of longing in his eyes. He walked around the table and leaned down. Then he placed a kiss on her cheek.

She reached up and touched his cheek. "I miss you too."

After work, Mel went to the mercantile to finally buy some pantry supplies and food for the next day or two. The owner sent a boy to help her carry everything home. Between the two of them, she only had to make one trip.

Once the boy set the things on her counter, she gave him a few coins and closed the door behind him. A few minutes later someone knocked on her door.

"Helen!" she greeted her sister.

"Ira is in town. Can I stay with you for the weekend?"

"Absolutely. Why don't you join Alex and me, and Bethie and Hawk for supper at Alex's tomorrow night?"

"We would love that. Let me put my things down and take the horse to the livery. Then I'll be back."

"Would you mind stopping by Alex's to let him know you will be coming tomorrow."

Helen agreed and left.

Mel took her things upstairs to the spare bedroom, suddenly very excited to have her sister stay for the weekend. It would be nice to see her some. She wondered how much longer before Ira would finally propose.

When Helen returned, she got a partial answer. "He is headed out to Papa's tonight to ask for permission to marry me."

"When do you think you'll get married?" Mel asked.

Helen's eyes lit with excitement. "I'm hoping he asks me this weekend. If so, then we would get married in four weeks, on April twelfth. He has to get set up in Camp Verde by the first full week of May."

"So soon? We will miss you."

"I know. I will miss everyone terribly. But the mail service is good. And we can come home every now and again."

Mel gave her a big hug. "I'm so happy for you."

"Well, it's not official, yet."

"It will be soon."

Helen and Mel prepared a meal together and talked late into the night. Mel mostly listened as Helen talked about her dreams for her life with Ira. It was nice to see her youngest sister grown up and very happy.

CHAPTER 25

Mel woke to the smell of bacon. Bless her sister for making breakfast. She washed up and donned a simple brown dress with a high collar. Then she went downstairs.

"Morning, Helen. You didn't have to make breakfast."

"Morning. I was up early and thought you could use a treat."

Mel went over to the coffee pot and poured herself a cup. Helen shooed her out of the kitchen, so she took a seat at the table.

"What had you up so early?"

"I think Ira is going to propose today."

"Did he stop by?"

"No. It's just a feeling. Unless Papa didn't give his blessing." Helen's eyes went wide as she set a plate of bacon, potatoes, and eggs in front of Mel. "What if he didn't?"

"The only way Papa would not give his blessing is if the man has some dreadful character flaw. And if that were the case, Papa would have made you stop seeing him some time ago."

Helen let out a sigh as she sat down at the table.

Mel said grace before they started eating.

"Does Ira have a house here?"

"No. He stays at the boardinghouse. Why?"

Mel smiled. "We should go shopping this morning,

then. Let's pick up some things you will need for your new home."

Helen's cheeks turned red. "I had not considered that I should be doing that."

"Never you mind. We'll get you started today. I'm sure Mama and Papa will help with some things too."

When they finished cleaning the dishes, they headed to the Brooks Brothers store at Mel's recommendation.

"They have a bigger selection of home goods and furnishings than the mercantile," Mel said as she held the door open for Helen.

"Oh!" Helen exclaimed as she stepped into the shop. "So many things."

"I would like to buy you a nice set of dishes," Mel said. "It will be my wedding gift to you."

"Mel, isn't that expensive?"

"I have plenty of money in the bank. That's a nice benefit of working as an attorney."

They walked along the counter and found the display racks of dishes.

"Morning ladies," Caleb Brooks greeted them. "What can I help you find?"

"A porcelain dish set for my sister," Mel replied. "She is getting married soon."

"How many place settings?"

"Four should be enough," Helen said.

"Eight," Mel said. "It's my gift to her, so let's plan for the future."

Caleb showed them all the patterns available with eight place settings. Several sets also came with matching serving dishes.

"Oh, I really like this pink rose pattern," Helen said. "And this yellow rose reminds of me of our old ranch."

"The pink set comes with more dishes," Mel said.

"Then the pink it is."

When Caleb started to say the cost, Mel shook her head and put a finger to her lips. Then she whispered, "I don't want her to know how much it is. She won't accept the gift."

Caleb nodded and scratched the total on a scrap piece of paper. Mel did not have that much money on her, so she set up an account and agreed to pay off the balance on Monday afternoon.

"Can you package the set so it can be shipped? She and her future husband will be moving out of town before they have a chance to use them."

"Of course," Caleb agreed. "Is there anything else you would like to see? I can start a list of items that your sister likes that way if other family members would like to purchase gifts for her wedding, they can stop by and pick something from the list."

"That would be wonderful," Helen said.

After another hour, Helen picked out several pots and pans, a table and chairs, some oil lamps, a bed, and linens. It was half past eleven by the time they left the store.

"Thank you so much, Mel. That was so much fun. Promise me you will do something similar for Bethie. It will help her feel like you approve of her relationship."

Mel was taken aback. "Does she think I don't approve? Alex and I invited her and Hawk to supper tonight."

"She's worried that you think he isn't good enough."

"He's been a friend to us over the years. How could I not approve?"

"I'm just telling you how she feels. It doesn't have to make sense to us."

"Alright. I will make a point of treating her to a day like

this soon."

When they arrived back at Mel's house, Ira sat on the front porch with a picnic basket in hand.

"I hope you haven't eaten lunch yet," he said. He placed a kiss on Helen's cheek.

"No, we haven't."

"If you don't mind, Miss Larson," he said to Mel, "I would like to steal your sister away for a few hours?"

"Please do."

Mel watched from the porch as Helen took his arm and followed him to the town square. Then she unlocked her door and went inside. She was not hungry, so she skipped lunch and sat down on the velvet sofa with her spectacles and a good book.

Helen returned around three. Her face was flushed, and her eyes shone with excitement. She held out her hand to Mel. "He asked me."

"That is a lovely ring," Mel said as she studied the simple gold band with a small ruby in the center.

"It was his grandmother's ring."

"Are you firm on the April twelfth date?"

"Yes. As it turns out, he needs to travel to Camp Verde on the fourteenth, so we would have a day together. Then he will come back the following week to collect our things and me, of course. He said to thank you for the dishes."

"Of course. When will you tell Mama and Papa?"

"I was hoping we could have them over here after church on Sunday?"

"Better yet, let's invite them to Alex's home. He says he has a large dining room."

"You haven't seen it yet?"

Mel shook her head.

"You should go over a little early tonight and ask him

about it. I would not want to impose."

"I think I will. It would be good for me to familiarize myself with his house before the rest of you arrive, if I am to act as hostess."

"We should invite the whole family, if Alex has enough room for us all."

"Let's start with Mama and Papa. Then we can have a big to do at the ranch next weekend."

Helen and Mel went upstairs to get ready.

"I can't decide," she said holding up two dresses for Helen to inspect. "The emerald or lime green?"

"Emerald." Helen flipped through her two dresses besides the simple work dress she wore. "I don't have anything nearly as fancy. Will I be under-dressed?"

"The pale blue brings out the color of your eyes and makes your hair look golden. You should wear it. And don't compare yourself to anyone else. I'm certain that Ira doesn't."

They finished dressing and fixing their hair. Mel studied her appearance in the mirror, certain Alex would be pleased. Then she headed over to his home around five o'clock. That would give her some time with him before her sisters arrived. Helen stayed back to wait for Ira.

She knocked on his door and suddenly felt nervous. A Chinese man opened the door and greeted her.

"Mr. Glassman will be down soon."

"You must be Zhao."

He nodded and then went to the top of the stairs. "Miss Larson is here."

"Which one?" Alex laughed.

"It's me," she called out.

He bounded down the stairs as he finished fastening a cuff link. Then he shrugged into his jacket and buttoned the top button. He glanced at the clock.

"You're early. You must have missed me." His cheeks moved up as he smiled.

"I did," she said as he pulled her close.

"I thought you said we should limit our alone time." He placed a hand on her neck and rubbed a thumb over her jaw line. "You don't make it easy on me."

She quirked an eyebrow.

"That dress." He ran a finger along the low neckline.

Her breathing shallowed at the fiery trail left behind his touch.

"Perhaps you should show me around before my sisters arrive?"

"Perhaps I should kiss you senseless and then show you around."

He lowered his lips to hers and kissed her sweetly, contrary to his implication. Still, it was nice enough to leave her lightheaded when he pulled away.

He cleared his throat. "This is the parlor."

"It's huge."

He laughed. "Is that the best you can do to describe it?"

"Well, it's elegant. I sense that you like dark wood, between all the dark wood here and at your office."

"Excellent observation."

"I'm not sure what I expected," she said turning around to study the room. There was a large, framed picture on one wall. She hurried over to it. In the bottom right corner, she found the signature.

"This is one of yours." She smiled as she studied it. "Where is this?"

He shifted his weight from one foot to the other. "It is the view from the valley south of Prescott looking at the mountain on a stormy day."

Her eyes traveled over the canvas. The dark sky was pierced with streaks of light shining brightly on the tall grass, giving it a golden hue. In the distance, rain darkened the mountain. The blues and grays he used to capture the storm clouds were the perfect choice to convey the magnificence of a monsoon storm.

"Did you get caught in that storm?"

He laughed. "Thankfully, no. By the time I set up, the wind carried the storm further away."

"What do you call it?"

He cleared his throat. "What makes you think I call it something?"

She turned to face him. She narrowed her eyes and searched his. "You do. Spill it."

He looked away. "New hope."

"And the one in your office?"

"New life. Come see the dining room." He tugged on her arm.

"Not yet. Why new life and new hope?"

His eyes begged her to stop.

She placed a hand on his bearded cheek. "Why?" she whispered.

He sighed and took her hand in his. "New life because it was the first painting I did when I came to Prescott to start what I hoped would be a new life. New hope because the monsoon rains bring me hope. Even when life appears dark and gloomy, the rain brings with it a freshness of new hope."

She smiled, thrilled that he finally opened up. She could see it was difficult for him to speak about his work out loud. She thought she understood. The way he painted he expressed much of himself in his work.

CHAPTER 26

Alex swallowed hard. He loved the way she pressed him about his artwork. It also terrified him to talk about it. Every time he did, he gave a little more of his heart away to her.

"Come see the dining room." He tugged on her arm again.

As he led her down the hall, she looked to the left at his den, instead of to the right at the dining room. She stopped.

"What is that?" she asked as she stepped into his den.

"Nothing," he said quickly as he steered her out of the den and closed the door.

"Is that something you started today?"

He could not talk about that painting yet. It was for her, but it was far from complete. He would call it "Oaks of Justice". It was the first time he tried painting purely from his imagination. So far, the only paint on the canvas was the thin sepia under painting to sketch out the idea. The oaks on each side of the canvas represented himself and her. At the top of the painting their branches intertwined. In the distance was the view from the top of the hill overlooking Colter & Larson ranch. It was meant to symbolize their strength as a couple and an eternal bond of love.

"Forget you saw that. This," he said as he dragged her forward, "is the dining room."

She glanced up at him. He looked straight ahead. When

she finally looked at the dining room, he let out a slow breath.

"It's lovely. I love the table and I find myself wanting to say it's huge."

He laughed. "It is. We can fit fourteen or more people around it."

She giggled nervously. "Is that how large of a family you want? It's a little intimidating if you do."

"I will take as many children as God sees fit to bless us with. But I hope it won't be that many."

"Oh, good."

"Now you can see why I wanted to host our dinners."

"Yes. Speaking of that, would you mind hosting dinner after church tomorrow? I know it's short notice, but Helen and Ira got engaged today and she wants to share the news with Mama and Papa."

His heart warmed. He would love to have the Larson clan dine in his home. "Of course. Do you want the whole family to come? I think we can accommodate everyone. Though we may have to set up a second table in the parlor for the children."

"I think just you, me, Helen, Ira, Mama, and Papa will be fine for now. I suggested Helen invite everyone out to the ranch next weekend."

"Let me mention it to Zhao to make sure he is prepared. Wait here."

Alex went to the kitchen door. Zhao confirmed he had enough food on hand to make a special meal for the next day, so Alex returned to the dining room.

He watched as Mel ran a hand over the smooth, glossy dark wood table. She seemed lost in her own thoughts. A small part of him hoped she imagined their children sitting around the table one day. She startled when she realized he returned.

"Your sisters will be here soon. Let's sit in the parlor while we wait."

She nodded and they headed to the front of the house. They sat in two chairs that faced toward the main part of the parlor.

"Judging by how large the downstairs is, I imagine there are quite a few rooms upstairs."

He smiled. "Yes. When I had the home built, I planned for the future, even though it seems it has taken longer than I hoped to find the right woman."

She reached over and held his hand for several minutes. "I like it."

Someone knocked at the door. Alex stood and offered his arm to Mel. Then they greeted their first visitors.

"Bethie, Hawk," Alex greeted them. He shook Hawk's hand while Mel hugged her sister. He liked having her by his side and thought that was what it would be like when she was his wife.

"We're coming!"

Helen's voice sounded from the porch before he closed the door, so he left it open.

"Helen. I assume this young man is Ira?" Alex asked.

"Ira Templeton," the young man introduced himself. He had a welcoming demeanor and firm handshake. He could see how the young man complimented Helen.

Mel hugged her sister and shook Ira's hand.

"Come now, if you are to be my sister-in-law, surely, I can give you a hug?"

"Of course," she said as she hugged Ira.

"Sister-in-law?" Bethie asked.

Helen held out her hand.

"Oh, it's lovely," Bethie said with a touch of sadness in

her voice. Alex wondered if she hoped to be engaged first.

"It was my grandmother's," Ira explained.

Alex had an idea. He would see if Rebecca had brought their mother's ring with her when she moved. If so, he would like to give that Mel.

"Come on in." Alex showed their guests to the dining room as Zhao finished setting out the dishes.

As they were seated, Zhao offered each of them wine, sweat tea, or water.

"Sweet tea?" Hawk asked. "Are you from the South?"

Bethie added, "Have you heard his sister? She has the loveliest accent."

"But you don't sound like you're from the South," Hawk said.

Alex rubbed his hand down his beard and cleared his throat. "When I went to law school in Boston, I found it more convenient to change how I spoke." It was not the whole truth. The day he left his father's home he vowed to be as little like him as possible, down to his manner of dress and how he spoke. He supposed sweet tea was one tradition he had not given up.

He and Mel accepted the red wine as did Bethie and Ira. Hawk and Helen both took the sweet tea.

Alex prayed over their meal and thanked the Lord for Helen and Ira's engagement. When he finished, Hawk took a sip of the tea.

"Whoa! You weren't kidding when you said it is sweet." Everyone laughed.

"Think I might go for the water instead."

"I like it," Helen said softly.

Alex liked Mel's sisters. Where Mel was sassy and spunky, Helen was soft-spoken and steady. Bethie seemed very kind, if not a little insecure. From the few times he interacted with Caroline, he thought she might be closer in personality to Mel, though there were still some strong differences.

The conversation turned to plans for the future. Helen and Ira shared about their upcoming move which prompted the quick wedding date.

"Mel bought us the loveliest dishes," Helen said. "We can't thank you enough."

He made a mental note to see what Mel thought about him purchasing them some silverware. He didn't want to go overboard or offend George and Maggie with such a pricey gift.

After dinner, Alex suggested the men have a drink in his den while the women talked about wedding plans in the parlor.

"I guess you beat me to it," Hawk said as Alex closed the door.

He was pleased to see Zhao turned his painting around. Hopefully no one would ask him about it. He poured each of them some whiskey.

"What do you mean?" Ira asked.

"I am trying to figure out when to propose to Bethie. I thought maybe tonight, but it didn't seem right to take away from your good news."

Alex watched the two men. "What about tomorrow after church? Mel and I were going to have her parents over, along with Ira and Helen to share their good news. Would you want to propose in front of family?"

"Only if it is alright with Helen and Ira."

"I'll ask her tonight when we are headed home, and I'll let you know at church."

"So, when are you going to ask Mel?" Hawk asked Alex.

He nearly choked on his sip of whiskey. "May I remind

you; we've only known each other for two weeks."

"Yeah, but you're not getting any younger," Hawk teased.

"It's obvious you two are meant to be together. At least that's what Helen tells me," Ira said.

"Still, it seems a bit fast, don't you think?" Alex asked. That was what he told himself.

"I know what George Larson would say," Hawk said. "Marry sooner rather than later. I think I've frustrated him by taking so long to ask Bethie."

"Really?" Ira asked.

"He did mention that he and Maggie had a very short courtship," Alex said. "Is he a romantic?"

Hawk grinned. "You've seen him with his wife, right?"

Alex nodded.

"Then you know the answer to that question."

"I would hate to disappoint him," Alex admitted.

Ira snorted. "I think you should worry more about disappointing Mel, than her father. He seems like a very good man that just wants to see his daughters happy."

Alex finished his whiskey.

"Do you know who I can talk to about buying or renting a house in town?" Hawk asked. "I'm staying at the boardinghouse, but I'll need to find something for Bethie and me."

"Talk to Frank Murphy. He'll find you the right place," Alex said.

As the other men finished their whiskey, Alex led them out to the parlor. The three Larson sisters laughed, and their conversation slowed.

"Ready for some games?" Mel asked.

"What did you have in mind?" he asked as he took a seat next to her.

"Well, I ran out of time to make up some topics for charades. What about twenty questions?"

"I don't know," Helen said. "It seems like the two attorneys might have an advantage there."

"Pish posh." Mel waved her hand in the air to dismiss her sister's concern. Then she winked at Alex.

"Mel, you go first," Helen suggested.

"I'm ready."

"Is it a person?" Alex asked.

"No."

"Is it an animal?" Helen asked.

"Yes."

"Is it found on a ranch?" Ira asked.

"Yes."

"Is it a cow?" Hawk asked.

"No."

"Is it a rattlesnake?" Bethie asked.

Mel frowned. "How did you know?"

"I'm your sister," Bethie said as she smiled.

Next it was Alex's turn. He chose a horse and the Larson sisters guessed it in three questions, with Mel being the final question.

"They were worried about attorneys," he said. They all laughed.

They played the game for several hours and everyone had a good time. Finally, Mel suggested they should head home as it was past eleven and they had church in the morning.

Hawk walked Bethie home and Ira walked Helen, leaving Mel behind.

"I had so much fun," Alex admitted as he led Mel to the door. Her eyes sparkled with life and joy.

"Me too."

"Can I walk you home?" he asked.

She hesitated. "I suppose so. It is rather late."

Alex grabbed his hat and walking stick, then he led her out into the cool night.

"It was nice to see Ira and Helen together," Mel whispered. "I think they are well suited and will have a very happy marriage."

He agreed.

As they neared Mel's home, he saw Ira still said his goodbyes to his fiancée, so he decided to say his to Mel a few houses down the street.

"Thank you for suggesting we have your sisters over." He pulled Mel close, resting his hands on her hips.

She placed her arms around his neck and stood on her tiptoes. Then she found his lips and kissed him. She tasted so sweet and felt warm against his chest. He kissed her back, reminding himself to keep his hands at her waist and to remain somewhat restrained. When she slowed the pace, he allowed her to end the kiss.

"I love you," he whispered.

She rested back on her heels but did not let him go. "I love you, too."

Then she laid her head against his chest for a moment before she released him. "See you tomorrow."

He smiled as his heart filled with joy. He watched carefully as she walked the last few feet to her house and disappeared behind the closed door. He really did love his sweet whirlwind.

CHAPTER 27

Sunday came earlier than either Mel or Helen wanted. Mel pulled herself out of bed and forced herself to wash up and don a dress. She did not put too much thought into it. Then she roused Helen.

As Helen got ready, Mel fried up a few eggs. She was not very hungry, so she kept breakfast as simple as eggs and bread.

She poured her and Helen coffee as Helen took a seat.

"We didn't stay up that late, did we?" Helen asked.

"No. Aren't you glad we don't have to cook Sunday supper?"

"Yes."

They both moved slowly until they stepped out into the chilly morning air. Mel was glad for her shawl.

They walked to church, as Mel remembered she was supposed to ask Helen about supper.

"Did Ira talk to you about Hawk and Bethie coming to supper?"

"Yes. He said Hawk wants to propose. I thought it would be spectacular if he did that in front of us and Mama and Papa."

"Oh, good."

"I was thinking," Helen said. "I'm sure since they have been courting for so long, they would be open to a short engagement."

"I would think so."

"What do you think about Bethie and me having a double wedding? I really want to be here went she gets married, but I don't think I could make it back home in May."

"Helen, that is a fantastic idea. You and Bethie have always been close, so I think she would like it."

Helen took her hand and swung their arms, like they had as young girls. "That will leave you the last to get married."

"I suppose it will." Mel pondered the words.

Her relationship with Alex was so new. Yet, it felt like she had known him for years. He had been mostly open with her, even sharing his heart about his artwork, something he had not done with anyone else. And she had been very open with him.

She would not mind a quick and short engagement herself, despite the short time she had known him. Their hearts were entwined, like that painting she caught a glimpse of in his den.

Mel did not want to rush him. It was important to let him decide the tone and direction of their relationship. But she did hope he would not wait too long to propose.

When they arrived at church, Hawk and Ira conversed. Alex found her and asked her to sit with him.

"Hawk is going to propose at supper," he said.

"I know. I think Helen is going to suggest she and Bethie have a double wedding."

Alex smiled. "Care to make it a triple wedding?"

"Probably not, since I don't have myself a fiancée yet."

"Fair enough. Would you be amiable to having one soon?"

"Well, he would have to ask me to find out."

She was confident her smile told him all he needed to know.

Once church was over, she waited for Alex. He said he needed to talk to his sister about something important for a few minutes. Mama and Papa along with her sisters and their beaus headed over to Alex's house. Zhao would let them in if they arrived before they did.

"All set?" he asked as he offered her his arm.

"How is Rebecca doing?"

"Well enough. She mentioned she has been sick in the mornings. She misses Perry, of course. She thinks he might be home tomorrow, though."

When they arrived at Alex's house, her family waited for them in the parlor. Alex welcomed everyone then led them back to the dining room.

After Papa said grace, Hawk stood. He kneeled on one knee in front of Bethie.

"Elizabeth Larson," he started. "You know I love you more than fresh air and sunshine. More than anything else in this world. Would you do me the honor of becoming my wife?"

Bethie's cheeks grew rosy. "Yes, of course."

Then Hawk slid a ring on her finger and pulled her close for a swift kiss.

"But what will my last name be?" she asked.

Mel pondered that question. In all the years their family had known him, he was always just Hawk.

"As you know, I was captured by Indians when I was young. I don't know my family name. So, if it's alright with you, I would like to do something a little unconventional."

"Go on," Bethie replied.

"I would like to take your last name."

Alex leaned over and whispered to Mel, "Don't get any

ideas."

She held back a snicker.

Bethie looked toward Papa and Mama. Papa smiled and nodded. "I suppose I would like that. Though it will be rather unusual to go from Miss Larson to Mrs. Larson."

"Great. Alex has the necessary paperwork ready, so we'll get it filed tomorrow."

"You do?" Mel whispered.

"Anything for my future in-laws." He winked at her.

"One more thing," Helen said as Zhao finished setting out their meal. "What do you say to a double wedding on April twelfth?"

"Really? Are you sure?" Bethie asked.

Helen rounded the table to hug her sister. "Positive."

Mel looked over at Mama, who dabbed away a few tears. Papa held Mama's hand as a sheen coated his eyes.

"Yes!" Bethie responded. Then she looked to Hawk. "If that's alright with you?"

"I'm definitely in favor a wedding soon. Though we have our work cut out for us to find a home and get it set up while planning a wedding."

"Not to worry," Mel said. "Once we tell Caroline, things will be magically taken care of."

Everyone laughed as they dished up their meal.

"My heart is full," Mel said softly so only Alex could hear.

He smiled at her and squeezed her hand. "No triple wedding, love. But I do promise I won't let you be an old maid for too long."

She smiled back at him.

The rest of the afternoon was filled with plans for a double wedding at the ranch. April would be such a nice time of year for an outdoor wedding.

Finally, around four o'clock, Mama and Papa said their farewells to head home to an empty house. Mel saw a hint of sadness in Mama's eyes, when Helen said she would be staying with her for a few more days.

That was how life went. Each of the Larson girls were women finding their new lives with the men they loved. Mel wondered if she would handle that season of her life as well as Mama appeared to.

Over the next few hours, Mel and her sisters played a few games. Then Ira took Helen home.

As Hawk and Bethie left, Mel decided she should go too.

"Stay for a few minutes," Alex asked.

"I'm tired and have an early day tomorrow," she said.

"At least let me walk you home."

"I think I'll be fine. You've already done so much this weekend."

He kissed her softly on the lips and let her go.

CHAPTER 28

Mel smiled as she walked the few blocks home. From the distance, she saw the lamp lit in her window and no sign of Ira, so Helen must be safely inside.

Suddenly, she was knocked to the ground. The wind left her lungs as a man with stout arms straddled her.

"I told you I would kill you."

Westbrook!

Her heart slammed against her chest. He pinned her arms down on the boardwalk. He smelled of alcohol and sweat.

She kicked her legs and filled her lungs with air. When she was about to scream, he hit her hard across the face and then in the gut.

The air left her lungs.

Then he squeezed his hands around her neck. She clawed at anything her arms could reach. His arm. His face.

He loosened his hold and hit her in the eye.

Tears poured from her eye as it went fuzzy. She could feel it swelling shut. She pounded against his chest, but he was too strong.

All she could think about was how much Alex would suffer when she was gone. He would blame himself for this, but it was not his fault.

Then she saw Westbrook pull a long knife from his

waist band. He held it over her. All the graphic descriptions from his letters filled her mind. It was a horrible way to die.

His arms came down full force into her right shoulder. Searing pain caused her to scream out. When she did, he clamped one hand over her mouth.

"Shut up!" he growled.

The pain made her nauseous.

He took the knife and ran it down her right arm from her shoulder to her elbow, splitting her skin open along the way. He took his time.

The evil in his eyes terrified her. She tried to cry out, but his grip remained strong over her mouth. Was this what his poor wife endured?

He lifted his hand from her mouth, and she screamed as loud and long as she could.

He smacked her face again.

She saw him raise the knife high above his head directly over her sternum. She closed her eyes and prayed. *Lord, if it is your will, please don't take me home yet. Don't let Alex blame himself for this.*

———

Alex closed the door behind Mel. He poured himself a whiskey, but before he took a sip, dread washed over him.

Go!

Go, where?

Go, now!

Mel.

He grabbed his walking stick and ran out the front door towards Mel's house. A few houses down, he saw her on the ground.

Westbrook was over her.

186

Alex ran as fast as he could. He took his walking stick and turned it upside down so the handle would hit the evil man.

Just as Westbrook raised a knife above his head, Alex swung his walking stick with all his might towards Westbrook's head.

It made contact splattering blood in Mel's face.

Westbrook rolled off Mel and charged at him with the knife. He sliced Alex's arm. Then he came at Alex again. That time, Alex raised his walking stick to block the blow.

When Westbrook raised his arm again, Alex struck him in the head a second time with the walking stick.

A gunshot reverberated through the nearly empty streets as Hawk came up beside Alex. Westbrook grabbed his leg and scurried away.

Alex fell to the ground next to Mel. Blood was everywhere. Her blood.

"Let me see your arm." He recognized Helen's voice.

He allowed her to wrap something around his arm as he stroked Mel's hair.

"Don't leave me, Mel," he whispered over and over again.

Her eyes fluttered open. Her voice was scratchy and barely audible. "I love you. I'm so sorry."

Her eyes shut.

Then he gathered his love in his arms despite the throbbing pain in his left arm. He ran toward the doctor's office.

When he arrived, the doctor took her from his arms and back to a room. Alex tried to follow but he staggered as the rush of adrenaline left his body. He collapsed in a heap on the floor.

Someone helped him up and into another room.

"Is she going to make it?" he asked. He felt as if someone

had ripped his beating heart clean from his chest.

"Relax," a woman's voice said.

Then he closed his eyes.

Sometime later Alex woke. The scenes of the dark street filled his mind. He looked down at his arm. It was bandaged. He sat up.

Then he stood and walked out into the hallway.

"Where is she?"

The doctor did not argue with him but led him to Mel's room.

All the color was gone from her face. Her right eye was purple and swollen shut. There were angry red marks on the side of her face. Her neck. Her beautiful, graceful neck had bruises the size of Westbrook's fingers.

"Oh, God!" he cried out.

"She has lost a lot of blood. The stab wound on her shoulder will take some time to heal. Like you, she has stitches on her arm."

"Is she going to make it?"

The doctor led him to a chair by her bedside. "Time will tell."

Alex ran a hand through his hair. Then he stroked her beautiful red hair. It was matted with dried blood.

It was then he noticed Helen and Bethie on the other side of Mel's bed. They clung to each other, their eyes closed and lips moving. They were praying. He should be praying too, but no words would come to him.

"Please," he whispered over and over again.

He rested his head on her bed and held her hand in his.

"Alex." Helen nudged him. "Alex."

He lifted his head. Sunlight streamed through the window.

The doctor entered the room. "I've done all I can for

her. Her color is returning, so I recommend you take her home so she can rest in a familiar place. I called for Paul Lancaster. He will be here shortly to carry her home."

Alex nodded numbly.

When the giant of a man, Paul Lancaster arrived, Alex followed behind him and Helen to Mel's home. Ira and Bethie were already at Mel's home. Helen showed Paul to Mel's room. Bethie followed them upstairs. Ira suggested he sit on the couch. A minute later Paul returned.

Alex managed to thank him despite the numbness in his soul.

"The sheriff is here," Ira said. "To take your statement."

Alex nodded. He managed to relay what he saw. Then some of his fog lifted. "We need to go after him. I don't care if it takes every man in this town, we need to find Westbrook."

A purpose. It was what he needed to make it through.

"You should go home and clean up first," the sheriff said.

Alex glanced down at his clothes. Dried blood coated most of his shirt and vest. His jacket was gone. He could not remember what happened to it. As was his walking stick.

Helen and Bethie joined them.

"I think we should take her out to the ranch," Helen said. "We'll send Adam and Georgie back to help."

Alex's mind cleared. "Don't let your father come. He needs to stay and protect her if that animal shows up there."

"Ira will help us get Mel to the ranch," Bethie said. "Go home and clean up."

Alex nodded and headed out the door. As much as he would love to stay by her side, he needed to protect her from Westbrook. The best way he knew how was to hunt the sick beast down.

Once at home, he changed into a blue cotton button

down shirt and denim pants. If he still had his heart within his chest, he would have smiled. Mel would like that he bought some clothes appropriate for the ranch.

After he changed, he headed down to the sheriff's office.

"I'm not sure you should come with us, Mr. District Attorney," the sheriff said.

Alex frowned. "You better believe I'm coming."

Harrold was there and pulled him aside. "I don't think that is wise."

"I don't give a fig."

Alex strode out of the sheriff's office where several men stood with horses. Thomas was there and handed him the reins to a horse.

Adam and Georgie pulled up next to them. They spoke with the sheriff and came back to where Alex awkwardly mounted the horse.

"Hawk is already on his trail," Adam said. "You got a gun?"

Alex shook his head.

Adam handed him a revolver. "You ever shoot a gun?"

Alex frowned.

Adam showed him the basics and then gave him a warning. "You point it at a man, you darn well better pull the trigger. Don't hesitate."

Alex nodded.

Georgie squeezed his shoulder. "We'll get him. Don't you worry."

Alex prayed they would.

CHAPTER 29

Mel woke up to the jostling of the wagon as it pulled to a stop.

"We're home," Helen said.

"What's going on?" She heard the fear in Papa's voice.

"Westbrook," Ira said. Then he spoke in hushed tones to Papa.

Mama whimpered.

"Baby girl." Papa's voice broke. He coughed. "I'm gonna take you in the house. You let me know if it hurts."

She tried to talk, but her throat hurt. She nodded instead.

Then Papa held her with one arm under her legs and one behind her shoulders. She lifted one arm around his neck.

She moaned. Everything hurt.

"Almost there."

Then Papa gently laid her down in her old bed.

"What…" Her voice sounded foreign, and the smallest of words sent fire through her throat.

"Rest now," Mama's soft voice came as she closed her one eye. The other had never opened.

Mel woke sometime later to soft voices around her.

"Westbrook."

"Adam and Georgie are on their way. Alex is with them."

"Alex?" she managed to say his name. She tried to open her eyes but only one opened.

Papa and Mama's faces came into view.

"Saved. Me."

"We know. Helen told us."

"Safe?"

"Yes, you're safe now," Papa said.

She moaned. That was not what she wanted to know.

"Alex. Safe?"

Mama refused to answer her question. "Rest now."

Mel closed her eye and relaxed.

The next time she woke, no one was in the room. Her stomach growled.

She tried to push up with her right arm, but searing pain flooded her body. She tried with her left instead and was able to sit up. Her one eye was blurry. When she felt her face, her eye felt swollen and puffy.

She moaned as she tried to get out of bed.

"Melissa Larson, what do ya think ya're doing?" Mama's angry Irish lilt stopped her.

She pushed her legs over the side of the bed and stood.

"Heaven help me," Mama said.

Mel nodded toward the kitchen and Mama helped her without further argument.

Her throat hurt, but she managed one word. "Day?"

"It's Wednesday."

Wednesday? She'd been out for two days?

"Alex?"

Papa joined them at the table. "He's still out on the manhunt."

She shook her head. Her stomach growled.

"I've got some chicken soup on the stove. Would you like some?" Mama asked.

Mel nodded.

"What. Happened."

Papa frowned and looked at his hands. "We almost lost you is what happened. No other details are important."

She frowned.

"Alex. Heart." She was trying to ask about his state of mind. Did he blame himself? Was he angry at her? Would he be alright? She had so many questions but could not speak.

Mama set a bowl in front of her and handed her a spoon. When Mel tried to reach for it with her right hand she moaned.

"Do you want to try with your left?"

Mel nodded. It was difficult. She spilled more than she ate. She acted like she held a mug and hoped Mama would understand.

"What a clever idea. I'll put your soup in a mug."

Thank goodness. When Mama handed her the mug, she sipped on the soup until it was gone.

"Tired."

Papa helped her back to bed.

Every time she woke, she asked the same thing. "Alex. Heart."

No one understood. They kept telling her he was on the manhunt. She did not care about the manhunt. She cared about the state of Alex's heart. She hated that she could not see him or talk to him. She needed to know if he blamed himself or if he was alright.

As the days rolled on, her vision began to clear. Her strength returned. She was able to move about the house and to the outhouse as needed. Her arm would take more time to heal. The bruises started to fade. The memories did not.

When her voice grew stronger, she gave up asking about Alex. Her family did not know much more than that he was on the manhunt with her brothers, the sheriff, Hawk, and several other men.

She worried about him.

Then Mel eventually turned her worry into prayers for him. For his safe return. For his heart. She prayed that darkness would not overtake his soul. She prayed that they would find Westbrook.

CHAPTER 30

Alex's arm hurt less after four days on the trail. He was exhausted but, he would not give up. They were close. He could sense it.

As he slid off his horse for the night, he prayed that Mel was alright. He could not return to her until Westbrook was in custody or dead. He would never forgive himself for any other outcome.

The posse totaled eight men in all. Sheriff Smith was the official law. The rest of them had been deputized, except for Alex. The sheriff was not sure it was legal to deputize the District Attorney. Hawk led the group as he tracked Westbrook to the northwest of town. Adam and Georgie, Mel's brothers, were among their number. A cowboy from the ranch named Jed and the wrangler Covington were there as well. It was clear from their interactions with Hawk that the three men were close friends. The last man was the sheriff's deputy Wilcox.

Adam and Georgie started a fire while Covington and Jed took care of the horses. Wilcox warmed up some beans, which Alex swore he would never eat again after he caught Westbrook.

"How you holding up?" Hawk asked.

"This is taking longer than I thought," he replied. "I'm worried about Mel."

"Westbrook is good at hiding. But I've got his number. His pattern doesn't vary, and I can spot his fake tracks right away now. We're close. I can feel it."

Alex nodded.

"Try to get some rest. If I thought you would listen to me, I'd tell you head back."

"Not happening."

Alex lowered himself to the ground and rested his head on his good arm. He fell asleep without any supper.

The next morning, he woke shortly before dawn. He found a place to relieve himself and just as he finished, he heard a sound behind him. He turned around to see the big bull of a man charge towards him.

He pulled out the revolver and shot. Two more guns went off, one to his right and another to his left.

Westbrook clutched his gut before a second bullet hit him between his eyes and knocked him on his back. Alex wasn't sure if the third bullet even connected with the man.

It was over. Just like that the evil man was dead.

Alex's stomach roiled. He turned and heaved the contents of his stomach onto the dry ground. Adam offered him some water.

"Looks like your bullet hit his thigh. Georgie's went into his gut and Hawk's was the kill shot."

Alex took a swig of water and swished it around in his mouth, then spit it onto the ground. He took a long drink and handed the canteen back to Adam.

His legs felt unsteady as he walked back to his horse. At least he could tell Mel that Westbrook would never be able to hurt her again.

If she had made it.

He leaned his head against the saddle of his horse as he stifled his sobs with his good arm. The emotions flooded over him in forceful waves. Fear and worry for Mel. Relief that Westbrook was gone. Anxiety over his decision to accompany the posse. Georgie and Adam looked on him with compassion. He figured they could imagine how they themselves would have reacted had it been their wife who was attacked.

As the sheriff and deputy took charge of Westbrook's body, the men from the ranch led the way home. When they finally reached the fork in the road that would lead them to the back way to the ranch or into town, Alex chose to go to the ranch.

He had to see Mel. Once he knew she was alright, then he could sleep for a week, if need be.

His mind kept trying to tempt him into fear. Fear that she might be gone. Fear that he would never get to become her husband. Fear that he would die knowing he was to blame for the loss of the only woman he ever loved.

The moon was a waning crescent, so they were forced to camp yet another night. As they sat around the campfire, Adam came over.

"Let me see your arm. My sister will kill me if I let you walk around with an infection."

Alex held out his arm and Adam removed the bandage. Alex did not look at it until Adam let out a sigh of relief.

"Looks like it is healing pretty good." He wrapped it in some clean bandages.

Alex returned his arm to the sling that held it steady to his chest.

"Your assistant said you shouldn't go. How much trouble are you going to be in for having been a part of this?" Adam asked.

"I don't know."

"Could you end up not able to practice law at all?"

"I will probably have to resign my position as District Attorney. And recuse myself from any case that I have knowledge of because of that position. But the only way I would be disbarred, is if the new District Attorney were to press charges against me for Westbrook's murder. If that went to trial…"

"But it shouldn't. We were deputized. Besides it was self-defense," Adam said.

"You were deputized. I wasn't. From a legal perspective, if they wanted to, they could pin the whole thing on me."

Adam frowned. "That's not right."

Alex nodded.

"Was it worth it?"

"I couldn't live with myself any other way. I also couldn't go back to Mel and tell her that Westbrook was still out there. So yeah, losing my job, possibly getting disbarred, maybe going to jail—I would do any of that to keep her safe."

Adam stood. "I gotta say, that's some pretty deep love for having met my sister right around four weeks ago."

Alex gave a half smile. "You said it. She's a force."

Adam laughed. "I'll be praying for good news."

"Thanks."

Alex laid down and fell asleep.

———

When Mel woke on Tuesday morning, she went out to sit in a rocking chair to watch the horizon for any sign of her brothers or Alex. The attack was a week and a half ago. Surely, they had to be on their way back.

Her voice finally returned almost to normal. If she spoke too loudly, sometimes she would get a tickle and then cough. She was still in a lot of pain, even though many of the bruises started to fade. Her eye looked horrific.

The doctor came out a few days ago to check on her shoulder and arm. He thought if she was careful with her shoulder, it might heal and function almost normally. He took out the stitches on her arm, remarking again how fortunate she was that the knife wound on it was shallow.

As had become her habit, she prayed while she rocked and watched for any signs of the man she loved.

A lone rider approached from the direction of Prescott. As he neared the house, Mel recognized him.

"Morning, Harrold," she greeted the Assistant District Attorney.

"Any word from Alex?"

She shook her head.

"I don't mean to add to your distress," he said.

Mel snorted. She no longer trusted him.

"But an ethics complaint was filed against Alex yesterday."

"By who?"

He looked away. The snake. It was him.

"An anonymous person."

"What is the accusation?"

Harrold narrowed his eyes and looked at her. "He tried to get himself deputized to go after the man that attacked you. It's very unethical. If Westbrook ends up dead, Alex will lose his job. Maybe even his license."

"Is what he did out of love for me more unethical than you trying to steal his job?" her voice was calm but steely.

"I would be careful, Miss Larson. You would not want to make an enemy of our next District Attorney, would you?"

Papa cocked his rifle. "I think you've worn out your

welcome young man."

Harrold glared at her for another few seconds before he turned on his heel and mounted his horse. He set a fast pace up the road and over the hill.

"Power hungry son of a—" Papa muttered under his breath.

Mel smiled. Alex was one of his and there was nothing Papa would not do for his family.

She went back inside to warm up. She still spent a few hours in the afternoon napping. Most of the rest of the day she sat by the fireplace reading. Helen brought out some clothes and her spectacles. She also brought word from Virgil to take as much time as she needed.

Mel was restless. Itching for a new case or something to distract her. But reading was the most she had energy for. She hoped Alex was safe.

CHAPTER 31

Wednesday morning, the men from the ranch had him up early. They all sensed that home was but a few hours away. Everyone was eager to be done.

When they neared the ranch, they first came across the cattle and cowboys in the far pasture. Coming at the ranch from this direction was not nearly as beautiful as coming from Prescott. He supposed home looked as good no matter what direction one came from.

A rider approached. It was George Larson. He first greeted Adam and Georgie and then Hawk before coming alongside Alex.

"She's on the mend," George announced.

Alex felt all the energy leave his body. She was alive.

Somehow, he managed to stay on his horse until he pulled it to a stop in front of the house. He slid off the side of the horse and turned to see Mel sitting on one of the rocking chairs.

She stood slowly and hobbled toward him. Her right arm was in a sling. She walked stiffly. When her face came into the sunlight, he let out a whimper. Her eye was purple. He could still see marks on her face and neck. She came to him and placed her good arm around his waist as she buried her head against his chest. He held her as close as he could with his good arm.

They both stood there for several minutes. He kissed the top of her head. She cried. He cried. He was not aware of the others around them. It was him and his Mel.

"He hasn't eaten in few days," he heard Adam tell Maggie. "He needs to eat and then rest."

"Has he been pale like that for long?" Maggie asked.

"Yes."

"He's gonna drive himself to the grave."

"Well, if you can pry him away from Missy, maybe you can keep that from happening."

Maggie came over to him and Mel. "Alex, Mel needs to rest now. Come inside I've got some stew warming on the stove."

Alex released his hold from Mel except for her hand. Then they followed Maggie in and sat down at the table. He ate a few bites of food, but his energy continued to fade steadily.

Somehow, he managed to follow Maggie back to a room and collapse onto a bed.

———

On Wednesday morning a few hours after breakfast Mel took up vigil from one of the rocking chairs again. Some riders approached from the direction of the herd.

"Papa!"

He came outside and followed her gaze. "I think it's them."

He hurried to the stables and saddled up his horse, then he rode out to meet them. When he neared enough to see them, he waved to her.

"Mama, they're back."

Maggie stepped onto the porch. She had been worried

about her sons and her future sons-in-law as much as Mel had been.

"Thank goodness."

The closer they got, Mel could make out each man. Adam and Georgie looked dirty and tired, but no worse for the wear.

Her breath caught. Alex looked frightfully pale and weary. He barely made it off his horse.

She stood and hobbled toward him, wishing she had the strength to run into his arms. When she made it to him, she buried her face against his chest and cried. His good arm circled around her. His shoulders slumped and his body shook with silent sobs. He was safe. *Thank you, Lord.*

Mama urged them inside for some food. Adam and Georgie declined as they were eager to see their families again. Alex stumbled into a chair.

"Westbrook is dead."

Mel let out a long breath. "Dead?"

"He can't hurt you anymore."

She had a dozen questions, but they would need to wait. Alex did not look well, and he needed rest. After he ate a few bites of food, he pushed his bowl away. Mama took him back to Helen's room, as Helen stayed at her house in town, in case the men went there first.

"He's out cold," Mama said when she came back into the kitchen. "I think some solid sleep and food will have him right as rain soon."

"Oh, good. Do you think I could sit with him?"

"If you keep the door open, I think that would be alright."

Mel stood and went into Helen's bedroom. She sat on one side of the bed resting her back against the headboard. She brushed Alex's hair back off his face.

"Thank you," she whispered as she closed her eyes.

"Melissa," Mama's voice was soft. "Let's get you to your bed."

She did not fuss but rose from Helen's bed and shuffled her way back to her own.

At supper time, Mama woke both her and Alex. She managed to walk to the kitchen without help. He waited there for her. Thankfully, much of his color returned. He smiled.

"I see you finally bought some ranch clothes," she teased him.

He laughed. "I did. Though I could probably stand to change into something else by now."

"You're tall like Will, so Hannah might have something of his that you could borrow," Mama suggested. "I'll go over after supper and ask."

"Thank you, Maggie."

As they ate, Papa brought up Harrold's visit.

"I'm afraid we might have some bad news. It sounded like Harrold Blankley is after your job."

Alex nodded. "I was afraid that might happen. I never quite trusted him. Something always felt off."

"He can't charge you with Westbrook's murder," Mel said. "From what Adam said, Hawk clearly fired the kill shot. All the men from the ranch back up that story. And they were all deputized."

Alex frowned and grew quiet.

Mel pressed him for some response. "Did you hear what I said?"

"Yes."

She reached for his hand, but he withdrew it. *Don't pull away.* Her heart begged him.

After supper, she sat on the couch in the parlor, and he

joined her. He put his arm around her but said nothing.

Papa helped Mama get a bath ready for Alex. She set out a shirt and pants from Will, then Alex went into Helen's room to clean up. When he came back out, his face looked sullen.

She could feel the distance and her heart broke. She wished she could crack open his heart and see what troubled thoughts brewed there. At least he came back and sat beside her again, with his arm around her.

He stared into the fire lost in his own world.

As the evening wore on, Mel grew tired and went to her room. She fell asleep quickly and prayed her nightmares would never return.

CHAPTER 32

The next afternoon, Alex took a paper and pencil and walked up the hill overlooking the lake. He sat down on the ground and sketched a picture of the ranch. What had Mel said about the place when he first visited? *It's the most beautiful place on earth.* He saw what she meant.

Nature had become a balm for him in the last few years. Gazing on God's beauty helped his heart when it was broken, like right then.

His jaw twitched. He shot a man. He should feel remorse but instead felt relieved. Westbrook would no longer be able to hurt Mel.

The cost had been high. When he made it back to town, he would resign as District Attorney. He hoped that would be enough to pacify Blankley his betrayer.

For a moment panic took hold of him. What if Blankley went after his license and he could not practice law? How would he provide for Mel? The law was all he knew. It was the only thing he ever wanted to do. Except maybe painting. But he couldn't make money off his artwork. Certainly not enough to provide for a wife and family.

He pushed the thoughts aside and concentrated on studying the scene before him. He sketched the perimeter of the lake, then shaded it to match the glossy reflections. He sketched the Larson home, then the Cahill's, and the Colter's. With the pencil, he scratched long strokes to represent the tall areas of grass. Shorter movements left marks like the shorter grass.

A shadow fell across the page. He looked up to see George Larson admiring his work. He quickly covered it up afraid of facing rejection like he had from his own father.

George held out his hand. "Can I see it?"

Alex hesitated as images of his father burning his paintings came to mind. George was nothing like his father. He reluctantly handed over the page.

George leaned against a large rock nearby, carefully examining the picture. It reminded him of how Mel looked at his paintings.

"This is really good. Mel says you like to paint. Will you make a painting from this?"

"I don't know."

George handed the picture back and scratched his beard. "I imagine you're struggling right now. Feeling like your life is out of control. Lots of unknowns about your future."

Alex nodded and looked away feigning interest in the herd on the horizon.

"It's a hard thing, killing a man. You did it in defense of yourself and Mel. For those reasons alone, you need to let it go."

He frowned. He hated himself for it. No matter how evil Westbrook was, Alex felt terrible.

"Something occurred to me this morning," George continued. "Don't know if one thought has to do with the other, but here you go.

"It occurred to me that the love you are desperate to find is not Mel's love, even though you have it. It's not mine or Maggie's. You have ours as well.

"No, I think the love you are looking for can be

summed up like this: 'For I am sure that neither death nor life, nor angels nor rulers, nor things present nor things to come, nor powers, nor height nor depth, nor anything else in all creation, will be able to separate us from the love of God in Christ Jesus our Lord.'

"The love you are longing for is one I think you already know—that is God's love. You might just have forgotten how incredibly big His love is. And that's alright. Many of us do when we are living through some hard times."

George stood and pulled out a paper from his pocket. He handed it to Alex.

"Just wanted to say all that and give you a chance to sit with those words for as long as you need."

George squeezed his shoulder then slowly made his way down the hill. Alex watched him the entire way until he disappeared in the shadow of his porch.

Alex unfolded the paper and read the verses George quoted to him. Then he read them again. The third time he read them, his heart broke, and tears began to fall.

All the years of feeling like he was unloved, he had always been loved. Not by his wretched earthly father, but by his Heavenly Father. A love so deep and inseparable. His present failures and pain could not stop God's love. The evil that Westbrook tried to inflict could not stop God's love. The magnitude of losing his job as the District Attorney could not stop God's love. His feelings of failing Mel and her father could not stop God's love.

He wiped his hand across his face. He closed his eyes and lifted his face toward heaven. Then he took a deep breath. Then another. He pictured the warmth of the sunlight against his skin like a hug from God. He was a little boy crying in his closet, hiding away from Solomon Glassman. Yet, he was in God's lap, held close to His chest surrounded with all the love of the One who created him.

He was as loved as any man could ever be. And it was enough.

Alex sat there for another hour. Then he headed back down to the ranch. It was time to go home. Time to face whatever would happen with his job. Time to figure out a way forward. Time to determine when he would ask Mel to be his wife.

Maggie had cleaned his clothes and set them on Helen's bed. So, Alex changed out of the borrowed clothes and back into his own. Then he looked for Mel. He found her outside walking close to the lake.

"Hi," she greeted him with a smile.

"Hi."

He took her hand in his. "You seem to be walking better today."

"I am."

He turned to face her. She looked up at him and he smiled.

"I like your smile," she whispered.

"How do you even see it with my big beard?"

"Your cheeks push up and little lines form around your eyes which glint like the summer sun."

He laughed. "You are quite poetic."

She shrugged.

His eyes searched hers.

She cleared her throat and looked away. "You're going home."

He ran his fingers down the side of her face. She looked at him again. "It's time to face whatever comes."

"I want to go home too. Helen is still at my place, and she can help me for a few more days until I'm fully recovered."

He smiled. "I would like to have you nearby."

"Take me home, Alex."

Her words stirred that longing in him again. He wished he could take her to his home.

"Alright, let's see if your father has a good solution for how to get you there. I don't think it would be good to share my horse."

"I wouldn't mind." She winked at him. "It would give me an excuse to hold on tight to you."

He let out a shaky breath. "As good as that sounds—"

"I know, it's probably not good for my health."

He led her back down to the ranch. Within an hour, George helped Mel into the back of the wagon surrounded by some blankets and a pillow. Alex rode beside the wagon.

"Have I told you that you look good in ranch clothes?" she said.

Alex's eyes went wide. "Your father is right there."

"I know. I do think we might make a rancher out of you yet."

He laughed.

"I've been thinking," she said. "I think I might take a longer break from Pittman and Associates. I have some money saved up and can afford to take more time off."

"Won't you get bored."

"I don't know. I'm considering if there might be another law firm in town that could use a good trial attorney who is willing to learn and study like crazy."

He quirked an eyebrow. "Anyone I know?"

"I think you might know him pretty well."

He smiled. If that was her way of saying she wanted to work with him, he would move heaven and earth to make it happen.

Then an idea formed. Slowly a smile spread across his

face. If that wasn't the most romantic idea he ever had. Not everyone would think it romantic, but Mel would.

"I see the wheels turning, Mr. Glassman."

George pulled the wagon to a stop. He shook his head at them both as he moved to the back of the wagon to help Mel.

"You two remind me of me and Maggie at your age. Well, at Mel's age. You are a little old, Alex."

Alex dismounted the horse and held out his hand as Mel scooted to the edge of the wagon bed.

"But not too old for your daughter?"

"Not if she chooses you."

"I'm right here."

"We know," Alex and George said at the same time.

George helped Mel into her house. Alex came in for just a minute to say his goodbyes. Then he left and returned the horse to Thomas before going home. With any luck he could set his plan into motion starting the next day.

CHAPTER 33

"One week to go," Mel said to her sisters as they gathered around her table.

"Not to worry," Caroline said. "The dresses are done and waiting for you to pick them up from Sophie's shop. We'll head out to the ranch on Thursday. That will give us all day Friday to set up everything that is needed."

"Where are we all going to stay?" Bethie asked.

"Georgie agreed to take my children, so Thomas and I will take one of your rooms. Then two of you will have to double up."

"You know we won't get any sleep the night before our wedding," Helen said.

"Then maybe you and Bethie should share a room," Caroline suggested.

"Where are we going to put Alex?" Mel asked.

"Hmm." Caroline tapped a finger to her temple. "Too bad you aren't already married to him. It would make things easier."

"I think a proposal still comes before a wedding," Bethie teased.

"Has he?" Helen asked.

"No, not yet."

The three of them shared a conspiratorial look which made Mel very nervous. Before she could ask about it,

Caroline took control again.

"Adam's girls can double up, so that would leave us with a room for Mel at their house and a room for Alex at Mama and Papa's house."

"Maybe put Alex at Adam's house. The two of them seem to be friends. And I don't want to miss spending any time with the three of you."

"Alright. Alex goes to Adam's house."

"When does Ira get back?" Bethie asked.

"Wednesday at the latest. He promised. Mr. Harrison assured me there would be no close calls, like when Perry and Rebecca got married."

"Good," Caroline said. "That was very stressful."

Mel smiled despite a pang of nostalgia. The Larson sisters were all grown women, moving forward into lives with the men they loved. They would be spread out over Arizona. She hoped they would keep in touch no matter where life led them.

"Mel, flowers?"

"Right," she quickly recovered. "Martha Stanton says she has several red roses in bloom already and that we are welcome to use as many as we'd like."

"You'll pick them before we head out on Thursday?"

"Yes."

"Is Alex going out with us on Thursday?"

"Of course."

Since he was no longer the District Attorney, Alex went back to his private practice full time. As the owner, he chose to close the office on Thursday and Friday next week. He already let his clients know so there would be no surprises.

Her heart hurt for him that his dream of being the District Attorney ended so abruptly. She would ask him about it when they went to dinner that night.

Caroline continued on with her long list of plans. She was a harsh task master and Mel kind of wished she could elope just to avoid all the chaos when it came her turn to get married.

Finally at four o'clock Caroline and Bethie left.

"You need to get ready," Helen said. "You should wear your new dress."

"The bright blue one?"

"Yes. You look amazing in it."

Mel hurried upstairs and changed into the new dress. She finished fixing her hair as she heard Alex's voice downstairs.

"Is she ready?" he asked.

"Almost," Helen said. Mel had to strain to hear what else she said. "The real question is, are you?"

Mel frowned. Something was afoot.

She tried to walk down the stairs quietly, but one of the stairs squeaked loudly giving her away. She stepped into the parlor.

Alex smiled as his gaze traveled from her hair to her toes and back again. "Stunning."

His eyes said much more than his words.

"I hope you don't mind, but I need to stop at the office on the way to dinner."

"Oh. Didn't you just come from there?" she asked.

"No. I worked from my den this afternoon."

"Alright."

He led her down the street. He slowed as they stopped in front of his office. A large canvas sheet covered his window.

"Alex, what is going on?"

"No questions, or you'll ruin it."

She scrunched up her nose.

He took both of her hands in his. "Mel Larson, from the moment I met you I fell in love with you. You are the most amazing and talented woman I have ever met. I knew when it came time to ask you the most important question of your life, it would require something special.

"You see, it is not just one question, but three."

Mel glanced out of the corner of her eye. A crowd of people gathered around them.

"Pst. Over here," Alex said. When she looked at him, he went down on one knee.

"Mel Larson, my first question is, will you be my partner and my equal at our law firm?"

The canvas cover dropped from the window to reveal a sign. "Larson and Glassman, Attorneys at Law."

"You put my name first?" she asked as her breath caught in her throat.

"The only place you will ever be in my life is first."

"Yes. I will be your business partner." Her faced warmed.

She looked around at the crowd and realized it was her entire family. Mama and Papa. Georgie and Emmy and their children. Adam and Julia and their girls. Caroline and Thomas and their three children. Bethie and Hawk. Helen and even Ira. Virgil and Eleanor. Rebecca and Perry and her son.

"What?"

"No questions, remember."

She nodded.

Then he started another speech. "As I said, I have loved you from the first day I saw you. You were a little slower, lagging behind a few days."

He winked at her, and she giggled.

"It's a little scary if you look at our relationship on paper.

It seems very fast. Yet, in my heart, it has felt very slow. I have waited a very long time for you.

"Mel Larson, will you marry me?"

"Yes. Of course. Yes."

He slid a gold ring with sapphires and diamonds onto her finger. Then he stood and took her hands in his.

"One last question my love."

Pastor came and stood by them facing the crowd.

"What?"

"No questions, counselor," Alex teased. "My last question is, will you marry me now? Tonight? In front of all these people?"

"What? Now?" Her heart raced. "Now?"

Papa spoke up. "Say yes, Melissa."

"Well, I supposed now would be a really good time to honor my father. Yes, I will marry you now."

Alex whispered so only she could hear. "I'd like to kiss you now, but I'll wait just a little longer if you don't mind."

As the sun lowered in the sky, Mel and Alex said their wedding vows in front of their families and friends and in front of their firm. When pastor pronounced them husband and wife, Alex kissed her with gusto. Her family cheered.

When he stopped kissing her, she breathlessly whispered, "Did that just happen?"

"It did, my wife. I do have one more question," he said as he led her toward the church for their reception. "Do you want to be called Ms. Larson or Mrs. Glassman?"

"How about Ms. Larson professionally and Mrs. Glassman the rest of the time."

"I can agree with that."

The rest of their friends from church joined them at the reception. They ate and laughed and danced. Then after Alex mentioned it was getting late for the third time, she took the hint. He escorted her to their home.

"What about my things?"

"Your sisters packed everything up before going over to the reception. Zhao has already delivered everything to our bedroom."

She shivered in anticipation.

CHAPTER 34

Alex swept her off her feet and carried her into their home. He set her down once they were inside. The fireplace glowed in the parlor, as did several lamps.

Then he led her upstairs to his room.

When he opened the door, she stopped. Candles cast a soft glow reflecting light from the mirrors of her vanity.

"How did you orchestrate all of this?" she asked.

He was proud of himself and could wait a few more minutes for their wedding night to start. Maybe.

"The ring is my mother's. Turns out Rebecca had saved it, thinking that she might give it to Josiah when he was older. But when I asked for it, she agreed wholeheartedly that it should belong to you."

He kissed her full inviting lips softly, but she put a hand on his chest and pushed him back.

"That's the ring. What about the rest of it?"

"The firm was one hundred percent my idea. I asked Virgil if he would mind if I stole you away. He said he figured when you didn't come back to work you would probably end up working with me."

He lowered his head to kiss her again, but she turned her head away. He trailed kisses along her neck. She moaned.

"My family?"

"That was easy. All I had to do was mentioned the idea

to Caroline who then told Bethie who told Helen, and well your whole family. Your sisters said they didn't think it was fair that you should be the last to marry."

He started unbuttoning her dress.

"That's why Helen suggested you get a new dress last week. Darn it. It has a lot of buttons."

Mel smiled but let him continue to struggle with the buttons. "What else did my sisters say?"

"It was their idea to propose and marry you all at one time. Caroline said it was probably better for a quick engagement."

He kissed her neck as he undid the last button. She tasted so good.

"What man doesn't want to hear that his future wife wants a quick engagement?"

She started unbuttoning his shirt. He swallowed hard.

"Enough talking," she said. "Kiss me like I'm your wife."

Alex happily kissed her and took her to his bed.

———

The next morning Mel woke. She opened her eyes and looked around the room. She smiled and rubbed a hand on Alex's back. He was real.

"Morning beautiful," Alex said as he rolled onto his side. He played with a strand of her hair.

"Did we really get married yesterday?"

"Yes. A whirlwind wedding for my fiery whirlwind," he said.

He sat up. "I'm starving. You want some breakfast?"

For a moment she wondered if he was still up to something.

He jumped out of bed. Her blood raced at the sight of

his back.

He tossed a nightgown to her. "Put it on."

"My aren't you bossy?"

He donned some pajamas and then held up a new robe for her. "Come here."

She did and he helped her into the robe.

"Alright. I've got one last surprise for you, but it's downstairs."

"So far I've really liked all of your surprises."

"Good. Come on."

He took her hand in his and led her downstairs. The polished wood floor was cold on her feet. Then he led her to his den.

"Close your eyes."

She did as he asked. Then he opened the door and led her into his den.

"Open them."

She did.

"It's lovely."

Her eyes roved over the painting. Two large oak trees stood on each side of the painting. At the top, their branches intertwined forming a protective frame around the ranch nestled in the valley below. The brush strokes were more fluid than his other work. The light almost glowed off the canvas.

"What do you call it?"

"Oaks of Justice. There's a verse in Isaiah that says, 'They will be called oaks of righteousness, a planting of the Lord for the display of his splendor.' I went with justice because of our jobs. But the important part is that you and I are both doing what God created us to do. And by doing that, we stand united. Our love was planted by Him and the work He called us to do displays His splendor."

A tear slid down her cheek. Her husband was an amazing man. He reached up and wiped away her tear.

"I thought we might hang it in the office so we can both be reminded of the reason why we do the work that we do."

"I would like that very much," she said.

EPILOGUE

Prescott, Arizona Territory
December 25, 1892

Mel smiled and grasped Alex's hand, still as in love with him nineteen years later as she had been when they first married. Her children were rather wound up this morning, but it was Christmas Day after all.

Keri, her oldest was the most reserved of them. At seventeen she tried to bring some order to the chaos. "Settle down. I won't hand out the gifts until you do."

Alex laughed. "She's going to be a very reliable mother."

"Please, let's not rush her into that responsibility."

"Don't worry, we won't. I think she is going to follow in your footsteps."

"Oh? She hasn't said anything to me."

Alex winked at her. "Shh. You'll miss watching them open their gifts."

Keri handed out a gift to the youngest first. Eight-year-old Amelia smiled when she opened the new hair combs.

"Oh, Mama, can I wear them now?"

"Yes, come here." Amelia sat on her lap as Mel took out her wild pig tails. She brushed her fingers through Amelia's unruly red hair. Then she placed a comb on each side.

Amelia spun around. "Papa, do I look grown up like Mama?"

"Almost, sweetheart. You look as pretty as her."

"Thank you." She gave Alex a big hug around his neck before she sat down.

Keri handed Clinton, who was ten, and Archie, who was twelve, each a gift. They tore into the paper at the same time. Despite their two-year age difference the brothers liked to do almost everything together.

Mel smiled. She wondered if they would become ranchers like their grandpa or attorneys like their father. It was hard to tell as their interests vacillated between the two.

"Ropes!" the boys shouted. "Do you think Grandpa will teach us how to rope cattle?"

At seventy-four, Papa's health was in decline. Most days his arthritis limited his movements to around the house. He rarely rode any more. It was hard watching him grow old.

"I think you might have to settle for Uncle Adam teaching you while Grandpa tells you how," Mel said.

"Or Aunt Julia," Alex said. "I think she might be the better roper."

Mel laughed.

Keri handed a gift to fifteen-year-old Sadie. It was getting harder to know what to buy for the children as they grew ever closer to adulthood. She thought Alex really came through with his gift for her.

"A violin?" Sadie lifted the instrument out of the velvet-lined box. She held it up to the light. "Oh, thank you!"

She ran to hug both of them.

"There's a young couple that moved to town that are advertising music lessons. You can start the second week in January after school gets out for the day," Alex said.

Sadie's golden-brown eyes sparkled. Somehow, she ended up with blond hair, where the rest of her siblings either had red hair or brown hair like their parents.

"Keri, it's your turn," Sadie said. She found the gift for Keri and handed it to her.

Keri slowly and meticulously unwrapped the gift. So much like Alex, despite her blue eyes. She had his dark hair. She shared his mannerisms. Perhaps she would want to be an attorney.

Keri lifted the book from the paper. "Territorial contract law."

"Alexander," Mel groaned. "You didn't."

He winked at her. "Got to start her young if she hopes to be as successful as her mother."

"Papa, do you have a case that I can research for you?" Keri asked. Excitement lit her eyes.

Mel shook her head.

"I'm sure we can find you something to put that book to good use."

Keri held the book close to her chest for a minute before setting it down.

"Papa, here's one for you. It looks rather small."

Mel smiled as he shook the box.

"It's rather light. Was I naughtier than I thought this year?" he looked at her.

Her face warmed as she thought of a quick retort, but not something she would say in front of the children.

"Just open it," she said.

He meticulously opened the gift as if he might save the paper for a future gift. She shook her head. Like father, like daughter.

He opened the box and pulled out the printed post card. "What is this?"

"Read it," Mel said.

"New artist exhibit of western art. A. Glassman…" A sheen covered his eyes. "What did you do?"

"I sent twelve of your canvases to New York. They are on display at a prestigious art gallery. The curator would love to have more if you'd like to sell them. He says they are very popular."

He turned the card over and over. He read it silently to himself.

"I never thought they would be good enough for that."

"I know. That's why I sent them."

He gazed at her. "And here this year I was certain I could top anything you got me."

He stood and pulled her to him. Then he kissed her in full view of the children. Heat warmed her cheeks, but she kissed him back with the same tender love he shared.

The boys started making choking sounds, so she pulled back.

Alex scolded them. "Boys that is how you kiss your wife. Don't you ever forget it. Girls this is what you can look forward to from a man that loves you."

All five of them rolled their eyes. It was not the first time Alex gave them that speech, so reminiscent of her own father. It would not be the last either.

He released her and asked her to sit down. Then he retrieved the last gift from under the tree and handed it to her.

She pressed on the paper. It was something in a frame. Perhaps a new photograph of the children. She would like to have that in the office. They grew so much from the photograph two years ago.

When she tore open the paper, she frowned. It was a newspaper article. Then she read the words.

"Arizona's first woman attorney passes the bar."

Her heart pounded against her chest. Tears blurred her

vision.

Keri took the gift from her and read aloud. "Miss Sarah Herring, a former teacher in Tombstone successfully completed and passed her oral exam on December 9, 1892. Mama that was just a few weeks ago."

"Keep reading," Alex said.

"Making her the first woman attorney in the Arizona Territory. Miss Herring practices law at her father's firm in Tombstone."

"You win," she whispered to Alex. "That is better than the gift I got you."

"Oh, I don't know about that."

"Mama, will you take the exams?" Keri asked as her eyes lit with excitement.

"I don't know," Mel said. "I'm not as young as I used to be."

"You're only forty-two. You should," Alex said.

"Yes, Mama, you should," Sadie echoed.

The rest of the children said in unison, "Be what God created you to be."

"Well, how can I argue with that?"

Alex snorted. "I guess they do listen to me."

———

Two and a half months later, after hours of preparation with Kerri and Alex, Mel Larson took her oral exams as her entire family watched. Papa and Mama were there. Her sisters and brothers and their families. Her husband and five lovely children.

Before she started, Alex pulled her aside. "Do you know what today is?"

"The day I take my exams. That is why we are here."

"Yes, but it is also the day that you won the only court case you argued against me. Twenty years ago, today."

"It is?" She had forgotten.

"Remember, you have always excelled at everything you do."

She took her place at the lectern and answered question after question. Within the first few minutes, her nerves settled. She reminded herself that she had been doing this for twenty-four years. She was by far the oldest woman to go before the panel, but she was also the most experienced.

At the end of her oral exams, the bar announced that she passed.

"I have one request," she said to the panel. "I would like my name to read Melissa Larson-Glassman to honor both of the men in my life who have always encouraged me to be the woman that God created me to be."

The panel agreed and presented her with the certificate. She was finally a real attorney.

Papa came up and hugged her. "We're so proud of you."

Mama hugged her and then stepped out of the way to leave room for Alex.

Alex drew her into his arms. "I guess I'm going to have to get the sign maker out to change the name on our building."

"You can leave it for a few years. Let's see what Keri decides to do."

He whispered so only she could hear, "Now you and I are truly the oaks of justice, standing strong side by side for the causes of our clients."

Then he kissed her in front of the large crowd of people. Her heart overflowed.

Author's Note

When I first started working on the *Desert Manna Series*, I knew I would tell Alex Glassman's story. What I didn't know was who would be the best woman for him. In the early stages of my outline, I was originally going to pair him with Sophie Atwood. But the more I thought about what type of woman would appeal to Alex, I knew that was not the right fit.

After I finished the first draft of *Beauty for Ashes*, I went back and re-read the entire *Prescott Pioneers Series*. When I came to my descriptions of Missy Larson, I thought she was the perfect candidate for a love match for Alex. I dug through old notes and calculated ages and thankfully her age in 1873 would work.

I was also going to make Alex's story book 2 instead of book 3. The problem was when I decided I wanted Missy (Mel) Larson as the leading lady, I needed that extra year to make her age work out like I wanted, so I moved Grace and Joshua's story to book 2.

I had very little of Missy's character sketched out in the *Prescott Pioneers Series* other than her appearance and a brief scene at the end of *A Hope Revealed*, she could be molded into a rich character. I decided that Alex probably needed an intelligent and beautiful woman. So, I asked myself, what would happen if he fell in love with opposing counsel? Viola! *Oaks of Justice* was born.

The history behind women attorneys in Arizona is true. From the earliest days of the territory, the Howell Code, which was the foundation of Arizona laws, stated that legal representation must be a man. A few years after the territory was born, the law was amended to state that legal representation must be a man with some level of knowledge about legal matters. Within the first decade, several women were allowed to argue cases and represent clients, as long as they did so under the supervision of "a man with some level of knowledge about legal matters."

The story in the Epilogue about Sarah Herring is true. She was the first female attorney in Arizona. She passed her exams on December 9, 1892 and went to work in her father's Tombstone law firm. She later got married and moved her offices to Tucson.

My favorite part of the book was the opportunity to put a stuffy attorney on the ranch with the Larson family. I love how Alex's relationship with George filled what he lacked from his own father.

The biggest surprise for me in writing this book, was that I made Alex an artist. I had no intention of doing so. Yet, when I sat down to write the scene when Mel visited him after winning the case, I wondered what would happen if she actually looked at the painting on the wall that everyone else ignored. Then it just happened. Alex became a painter, which was a great way for him to express his emotions yet maintain his meticulous outward appearance.

The scenes about Alex's art were fond memories for me. I originally spent a year at a fine arts school in Philadelphia right out of high school. I loved painting landscapes and sketching back then. So, it was easy for me to write about the experience since I used to be an artist for a brief moment in time.

I hope you enjoyed Mel and Alex's story.

Karen Baney

––––

Want More Arizona Territory Romance?

Get a FREE novella featuring characters connected to the Colter Sons series! Plus exclusive updates on new releases, special offers, and historical insights from the frontier.

Subscribe at: books.karenbaney.com/larson-christmas

ABOUT THE AUTHOR

Karen Baney is passionate about writing stories full of flawed characters. She enjoys weaving together stories of second chances, redemption, and overcoming personal trials. As a transplant to Arizona, she loves researching the state's history and finding ways to seamlessly incorporate real history and real settings into her novels. In addition to writing and speaking, Karen works as a Software Development Manager for a Christian ministry.

Her faith plays an important role both in her life and in her writing. Karen and her husband, Jim, make their home in Gilbert, Arizona, with their two dogs, Bella and Daisy. Both Jim and Karen are active at Rock Point Church in Queen Creek, Arizona.

Discover faith-laced stories with characters who feel like lifelong friends.

Visit www.karenbaney.com to discover more historical romance series set in the American West. Follow Karen's writing journey and get behind-the-scenes glimpses of her research adventures on social media.

Facebook:	@AuthorKarenBaney
X:	@karen_baney
Instagram:	@AuthorKarenBaney
BookBub:	Follow Karen Baney for new release alerts

BOOKS BY KAREN BANEY

Historical Western Romance

Prescott Pioneers Series:

Step back in time to the wild, untamed Arizona Territory where survival depends on grit, faith, and the courage to start over. Follow three pioneer families—the Andersons, Colters, and Larsons—as they risk everything for the promise of a new life in a land that demands both strength and hope.

A Dream Unfolding
A Heart Renewed
A Life Restored
A Hope Revealed
Hidden Prospects

Desert Manna Series:

Sometimes the most beautiful love stories bloom in the desert. Set in the growing frontier town of Prescott during the early 1870s, these tender romances follow women rebuilding their lives after heartbreak and the unexpected men who help them discover that second chances at love are worth the risk. Set in Prescott, Arizona between 1871 - 1873.

Beauty for Ashes
Joy for Mourning
Oaks of Justice

Colter Sons Series:

Power, legacy, and forbidden love collide in this sweeping family saga set in the Arizona Territory. The Colter ranch empire has weathered decades of frontier life, but now family secrets and buried betrayals threaten to destroy everything. As five brothers—and one resilient sister—navigate the treacherous waters of love, loss, and redemption, they must decide what's worth fighting for. Set in Prescott and other locations within the Arizona Territory in 1887 - 1906.

The Reluctant Cattleman
The Roaming Adventurer
The Railroad Magnate
The Resourceful Stockman
The Restless Wrangler
The Resilient Bride

Larson Sisters Series
Meet the next generation! These delightful novellas follow the three daughters of Adam and Julia Larson from the *Prescott Pioneers Series* as they navigate love, courtship, and finding their own happily ever afters in territorial Arizona in 1886 – 1894.

In Love at Christmas
In Love with the Rancher
In Love with the Horse Trainer

Contemporary Romance

Vargas Ranch Series:
Love is in the air at the Vargas Guest Ranch & Resort near Wickenburg, Arizona. Meet the Vargas family—five swoon-worthy brothers and their cousins who live by their family motto: "We do not deviate from the Lord's plan."

These rugged cowboys run a successful working ranch and luxury resort while navigating the rollercoaster of finding true love.

Falling for a Fake Cowboy
Falling for a Real Cowboy
Honeymoon with a Real Cowboy
Falling for a Shy Cowboy
Falling for a Bossy Cowboy
Falling for a Smart Cowboy
Falling for a Humbug Cowboy
Falling for a Devoted Cowgirl
Falling for a Pregnant Cowgirl
Falling for a Cowboy's Legacy

Steadfast Love Series:
The *Steadfast Love* series follows a close-knit group of friends as they navigate the beautiful mess of modern life in the Phoenix area—workplace drama, complicated families, and love that shows up when they least expect it. These contemporary romances blend emotional depth with authentic faith, reminding us that even when life unravels, God's love never does.

The Heart I Rescue (prequel)
The Air I Breathe

Mama knew a secret about me...

My name is Sam Colter, and I am the misfit of my family.

Papa wants me to take over the family ranch. I don't think I'm the right son. Will I disappoint him or figure out how to run it successfully?

Then my life turned upside down when a journalist showed up. It was my job to protect the ranch and I failed. Worse yet, I find myself falling for the woman who betrayed me.

Is she the one? Can I forgive her?
Only the good Lord, and maybe Mama, knows for certain.
1887 is gonna leave a mark.

The 1880s and 1890s bring dramatic changes to the Colter family in Prescott, Arizona Territory. Family secrets, secret identities, and blind ambition threatens to tear them apart and stretches their faith to the limit. Will adversity bring them closer together? Or will family dynamics scatter them as these five brothers move into manhood? Will they remain Colter strong?

DESERT LIFE MEDIA

———

Desert Life Media: *There Is Life in The Desert*

Entertainment-first Christian fiction set in the Southwest, featuring redemption, family, and faith

Publishing clean, wholesome, and uplifting fiction since 2010

———

desertlifemedia.com

www.ingramcontent.com/pod-product-compliance
Lightning Source LLC
Chambersburg PA
CBHW051945220626
47052CB00004B/801